CW01501783

Introduction

Let's be honest - you probably can't. I wouldn't even bother. It wouldn't be any good even if you tried. Best put the pen down, turn around and go home. Give up while you still can. No point. None.

But what if it works?

What if you do put words on paper and it actually makes sense?

What if you write something and it is *good*?

OK then, what about just one sentence?

Let's try that.

Just one.

OK.

Now, what about one more?

Go on, write one more and then you can quit.

Go on.

Done?

Right, let's see.

OK.

OK, not bad.

Keep going.

I can see what you were trying to do there.

That's... that's pretty good.

Yeah, I like it.

I like it.

Now, shall we go again?

Bank Street Writers is a community who writes together, talks together, laughs together and drinks tea together. We are an unruly mix who have all thought we can't but still have.

Above all, we love to tell a story. This anthology is the result.

We hope you enjoy.

Our Work Online

Jack Nuttgens
jacknuttgens.wordpress.com/fiction

Tim Ingham-Dempster
inherentlyinteractive.weebly.com/fiction

Ollie Francis
olliefrancis.co.uk

Leanne Williams
preludesblogofwords.blogspot.co.uk

Sam Sharp
sharptales.wordpress.com

The Silent One
Jack Nuttgens

I lie in the grass, thinking about being dead as I await the Silent One.

An ant is the first thing to come along and it crawls up my neck, traces my jawline and works its way onto my earlobe, towards the hole, so I direct it away with a thought- *this way*. It doesn't tickle as much as it should; if I were alive it would be horrific, especially if it did make its way into my ear and I would hear it running round looking for food or materials, whirring, six legs, mandibles clacking. I'm still aware of what my body feels but it doesn't bother me, as though a neighbour is telling me, there's an ant on you. Thought you should know.

More ants come and they're not the one I want so I send them away, sweating acid to frighten them and overwhelm their sense of smell. I got the idea because they have acid themselves. My acid is mental but they don't know the difference.

Vultures come and I don't pay them any heed because I know they won't be long. Now that I'm dead time doesn't have such a grip on me, so I sense the king of the plains coming before he arrives, the great bald ugly marabou. I almost think he hasn't come when I see the shadow of his beak, all foot and a half of it, coming down from my head side. Lying on my back, there is up and down, but no in front nor behind. He snaps at me and I feel the bones in my neck move, my head hits the ground, comes up again. He hasn't got what he wanted. He's not the one I want so I roll my eye back, into my head, and fill where it was with a light that he can't look at. It's a rushed job, done too quickly, and I promise myself that I will be better prepared next time, let the magic seep out when needed and preserve my energy. I have plenty of spells, mechanisms, and if the scum doesn't bother me too much I can keep myself here for thirty days. The heat makes no difference. It's the maggots and the flies that eat you.

So when the lions come I'm prepared and I wait for them to stop fighting, the big male leaving his oldest son with a gash that may kill him, and the young lion runs away. The lionesses sit back as if they know what I am. Their husband comes to my leg first, even dead he can't look a human being in the eyes. He takes it in his jaw and is going to chew it off, he can't bite through the bones. The wind blows then and it takes some of the effect out of what I do, which is to direct some of my leftover gas through myself and sigh like this:

Aaaaaaaaaaaaaaahhhhhhhhhhhhhhhh

The lion takes a step back and puts his head up and for a moment I think what a stupid one, so intent on my leg he didn't notice but his tail starts going and he looks around, up and down my body then sniffs and turns around, going somewhere else. One of his lionesses mrrrs a question and he grabs her by the neck, shaking her.

Every corpse has the power to fart. The lions leave.

Then my distant sense make me aware of a high-pitched giggle in the night, as if my neighbour is now saying, don't you hear that, aren't you frightened?

I would have been, before. It's dark now and I know who it is and hope I don't have to use up, too much magic. It's not the one I want. My favourite of the scum has arrived. They can break your bones, easy, so I won't give them time. I lie patient, the magic builds best if you don't need it or if you don't think about why you need it. I lie as there is no hyena, *hehehe*, as if she isn't biting my stomach, trying to get it open, and the magic builds and slowly, without a sound, I raise my head.

The hyenas sit bolt upright and laugh to themselves, *hehehe*, and then they *run*. Run away, hyenas.

I don't want to think about how unnatural I've become, feeling like I'm lying in my own dirty bathwater. My thoughts are sluggish anyway, repeating themselves, and I can't stop thinking about the lions. I'll take cowardice any day if that's what bravery looks like.

It's quiet now. The night on the plains is usually so loud you can't hear yourself think.

The god I want is trying to wear me down. I have not forgotten my mission, but I will be distracted if I think about it too much. So she will make me sit through another day, and another, and maybe some people will find me, directed to me, not knowing why, and try to bury my body or burn it. They don't want my meat, but they are no easier to ward off than the scavengers. I think on the magic running in my open stomach and must be ready if they come.

The night changes and instead of dawning again it becomes a deeper night, and darker. I think then the god I want must come for me herself, the Silent One will come.

But instead she sends the nandibear against me. Towards the end of my life I started to think maybe they were real and now one is here and I really don't care.

It is not a true bear; not a true creature of the earth for its front limbs are made for rearing up and then dropping down again, able to stand higher than a human being on two legs, but without the balance to walk on them, yet the length is too uneven for it to walk on four legs comfortably. Its fur is white and the crusty skin beneath is pale pink, but I do not know whether this is typical of the species or unique to this nandibear. Its eyes are orange as far as I can tell. Its claws are too like hooks to be real. Something in its shape is familiar, frightening; I understand that there must be a whole menagerie of beasts like it, ready to dispose of anyone to stubborn to go the usual way.

It looks down at me, growling, and then it grips my head in one paw and rips and bashes me against the ground and then I really get confused and start trying to struggle, but my body will of course no longer allow me. At one point I feel wet so her mouth must be around me but I lose the thread of what's going on for almost a minute. She bites, twisting, taking my jaw in her own. She is too aggressive to stop. I know my head's all but off and I can't save it. It would be a waste to try.

I think, this nandibear doesn't know she only eats brains, then she goes away, leaving the rest of me for the other scavengers to clear up, half my skull and my jaw lying like eggshells to the side of my neck. That nandibear frightened me even through my unconscious shell; she had a calculated, almost demented fury and that set her apart. A predator is hungry, but that was a beast of nightmares, the kind of nightmares that show us what lies behind the thin curtain of the world when we're bold and naughty enough to peek.

I have missed my chance now. I allowed the nandibear to destroy my body too easily, and the Silent One will not come for one such as me; I was foolish to think otherwise. The scavengers will finish me off tomorrow, stripping away skin and fat, crunching open bones, sucking marrow, lapping up blood. I will see them all, the jackals and the dumb lions and the vultures, the Egyptian and the big friendly Lappet-Face and the one they call Ruppell's Griffon and the hyenas and finally the marabous themselves, seven or eight or nine of them. The ants will clean up.

Perhaps all these and more do come; I do not hear the sun come up, and my eyes were taken by the nandibear. My consciousness lolls and I cannot direct my thoughts until a time later. My body is gone, scattered to the winds. There was a fire on the plains, I know, but I was little more than bone by then anyway. In that time my memory was stuck in one groove, repeating the lines on my aunt's face when I told her what I intended; when I told her I wanted to confront the Silent God. I remember looking up at the stars, but it is possible that I am confusing that distant fire with the fire on the plains.

The Silent One is standing over me, as she has always been.

She does not deal with the bodies, that is for nature; for the ants and the clumsy lions. Her duty, or her hunting, is something different. I wonder if it was my body the nandibear broke, or my spirit.

She does not stretch out a hand, but looks at me for long enough to frighten me. She turns and I go with her. I wonder if others have been, or are, where I will go, whether my defiance has brought me a greater punishment. Most probably I go with the other unremarkable dead. I am not special.

My consciousness stayed after my body died, and even a little after it decomposed. Of that am I proud. But now I must go with the Silent One. I wanted to summon her to me, to challenge her, but she sent the nandibear for me instead. Now I go with her, but I go on her terms. I go on her terms.

Brain Bugs
Tim Ingham-Dempster

Bugs. I hate bugs. Not creepy crawlies. The other kind. Computer bugs. I used to be a programmer so I know what I'm talking about. I'll give you a quick example. I once worked on some financial software. Part of it was supposed to remove money from an account and put it into another account. Turns out it was only doing the first part but by coincidence the only amount that was ever used was 0 so it was never spotted. Until things changed and it tried to work on more than 0 money. Of course someone else spotted it before us. A lot of money disappeared before we figured it out. And that's the point really, bugs can be exploited. Did you know that the brain is just another type of computer? I never really thought about that until mine got reprogrammed.

I'm a bit of a nerd. I like old books. I used to love browsing strange old bookshops. Last year, around Halloween I was in one of my favourites. It's one of those places with doors that are only two feet tall and has more staircases than floors. I noticed a book with no title on the spine or cover.

It was a fairly mundane story, I don't even remember what it was about. For some reason I felt compelled to keep reading. As I read I began to feel a strange sensation in my brain. I felt warm and fuzzy. It was like I was completely safe and everything would always be alright. I felt like something was peering over my shoulder, reading it with me. Of course I bought it immediately.

That night I slept terribly. You know those nights where you think about every stupid thing you've ever done. I dreamed of a monstrous shadowy figure belittling me and humiliating me, telling me why I'd never amount to anything, telling me I was a failure, my life was a waste. By the morning I was a wreck. I remember how good reading the book had felt so I got it out and read it again. I felt better in no time.

My sleep was disturbed for about a week before the next incident occurred. I was walking down the steep street on the way to the station. Dodging the litter and dog shit I made my way down until I saw Jakey, the cat that lives at the house with the green door. I put my hand out to stroke him and he rubbed his head up and down my arm.

"See, someone loves you" I thought. "Except he doesn't." came the reply in my head. "He loves his real family more. He'll leave you as soon as they move. Just like your parents abandoned you. Just like everyone abandons you. Just like none of your friends helped you last year. Like all of the guys at the office who never remember you when they go out after work." I looked down through my watery eyes at the limp ball of dead fur in my hands. I, I hadn't done that had I? I'd never hurt an animal. I'm not that kind of person. No, it must have been an accident. I was so distraught I hadn't realised how tightly I was holding him. "Maybe I should tell someone?" I thought. "No, that would only cause trouble and it wouldn't bring Jakey back." I looked around. There was no one about so I quickly arranged his body behind the tyre of the nearest car and went to work.

Sleep got harder. Guilt now blended with my self-doubt until I was in abject misery. I lived in terror of someone finding out what I had done. I felt pursued, hunted, watched. I constantly felt that there was someone just outside the room. Reading, or even just holding, the book was the only time I felt safe and soon it became a daily ritual.

A few days later I was getting the lift up to my floor at work. I hate that lift. It's completely enclosed like a metal coffin. It stops and opens the doors at random floors when no one is waiting to get on or off. My boss got on at the next floor. "Oh hey, drop by my office later ok?" he said before going back to his phone. My stomach turned. Whatever had been following me was inside him. Something horrible was going to happen in that office. I could feel the malice radiating from him. I had to do something right now. It was just the two of us in here and his back was turned. Now was the time. I reached into my bag to see what I could use. My hand clasped something and drew it out of the bag. It was the book. I felt better straight away. Of course there was nothing possessing him, what a ridiculous idea! I felt the safety and comfort of the book flowing through me and knew that everything would be alright.

About a month later I was in an absolute state. I still felt guilty about Jakey and was constantly tormented by regrets and self-loathing. I walked home in the dark one day and felt the presence stronger than ever. I looked around but the road was almost deserted. Just me and a woman in front of me. I felt like a monster was pursuing me. Like the night itself was reaching out to grab me. I quickened my pace. I wanted to get home to the safety and comfort of the book. The stranger in front must have heard my footsteps because she looked around. Her face flushed and she sped up. What had she seen? I daren't turn around to find out. I sped up again. She looked around again. Her face paled and she broke into a run. Blind panic took me and I sprinted after her. She turned left into another road and the right into an alley. "Clever I thought, we'll get off the main street and hide till it passes."

She screamed as I entered the alley. "No, no, hush, quiet! It'll hear you!" I yelled but it didn't make any difference, she kept on screaming. There were only seconds till it would be too late so I rushed up and put my hand over her mouth. She tried to break free but I had my hand on her throat. Her screams were muffled but I could feel its presence getting closer and closer. Finally she stopped screaming but it was just beyond the alley now. It waited. I heard it snuffling. After an eternity it slunk away and I let her go. Her body slid to the ground. She didn't have a pulse.

The police didn't get close to me before I confessed a year later. In the mean time I was falling apart. Was it all in my head? Had there ever been a pursuer? I spent the next few months terrified of my own actions. I watched myself like a hawk. I spent every minute expecting to be arrested but it never happened. There hadn't been any witnesses and we had no connection what so ever.

It was the school that finally broke me. We were there for one of those "get kids to code" type events. I was running late when I arrived and the others were already in the hall giving the presentation to the entire school. I was walking up to the big, ornate, windowless doors when I felt the presence again. It was inside the hall. I couldn't go in there. It got worse. It was coming out to get me. I should block the door! I quickly dragged a bench across the huge doors but it just moved towards the fire doors. I blocked them in the same manner.

"Wait," I thought. "This is just what happened before. It's all in your head." I reached for the book. I was taking it everywhere I went now. I felt that familiar relaxing fuzziness sweep through my body and knew that I was safe from anything that could be in the hall.

Then the dread re-doubled. It hit me like a wave and the comfort of the book vanished. I staggered as I felt the mind behind the wall searching for me. I knew it would find me soon and that all would be over. I had to get out of there. I ran. When I finally turned around I saw the smoke pouring out of the building. I saw the flames starting to lick at the windows. I heard the screams of those trapped inside. Had it really burned the building just to get out and pursue me? Had, had I burned the building to kill it? I couldn't remember. I still can't. I felt relief though. At least it was dead and couldn't harm anyone else.

That night was the first night it spoke to me. It told me there had been no monsters. Just its voice whispering its siren song in my head. Poisoning my thoughts and prompting me at crucial moments. It had me so much in its power that it no longer needed to hide its true nature. It mocked me for my weakness and my failure. It told me how it had implanted itself in my brain when I first read that book. How the words created mental images and patterns of thought and feeling that had a mind of their own, using my brain to live. I tried to destroy the book but I couldn't. Even though I knew what it was I still felt that safety and euphoria every time I touched it. Any thought of destroying or removing it made me nauseous and wracked my body with pain.

I was working with it willingly now. It had trained me over the past months by flooding my body with indescribable pleasure whenever I did what it wanted and unbearable agony when I didn't. I didn't even know what were my ideas and what were its anymore. I arrived at the airport arrivals lounge with my laptop and plenty of time to work. I'd already written the software and tested it remotely. I didn't really need to be there in person for that part you understand. It was surprising simple to break into the systems and convince them that the runway was several hundred feet lower than it actually was.

The next part was the reason I needed to be there in person. It would take time to authenticate the video if I shot it at home but by standing in front of the live arrivals board while I explained what I'd done it would be immediately obvious that this was no hoax. After I uploaded it to every video hosting site and rolling news channel I found the nearest security guard and explained the situation. I was soon surrounded by armed police as the news started to spread amongst the people waiting for their loved ones' flights to arrive. A mob formed before I could be taken away and even the police tried to coerce me into saving the plane. I was beaten but didn't feel a thing as my system flooded with endorphins. As the camera crews started arriving the relatives realised there was nothing they could do but watch helplessly as the plane descended towards the tarmac far too fast. We had created the world's first live-streamed plane crash.

Eventually the police managed to manhandle me through the mob and I was arrested. That was its plan all along. It wanted me to be famous. It wanted attention and it certainly got it. The trial was quick since I had confessed. No one believed my story but it was clear to them that I was insane. That's how I ended up here in this hospital. Locked away for the rest of my life where it can't make me hurt anyone else. Or at least that's what they think.

It had one last task for me to perform. It was going to use my notoriety. It made me write a new story. One that my name would make famous. A story that would infect the reader with its offspring. This story. The one you just read. It's inside you now. Can you feel it? That little itch in the back of your brain. That feeling that someone is standing just behind you or just outside the room. You'll start to notice its thoughts slipping into your own soon. I'm sorry. I'm so terribly, terribly, sorry. It made me do it.

On Edge
Gareth Madgwick

"So, why do you think I'm here?"

Trisha was so matter of fact as she stood there, arms folded. Terry held his cup in his hand, staring down at it. He could see the ripples forming circles, reminding him of the dramatic moments in a long ago film. His attention was always on the tiny, unimportant things.

"Well?"

He shook his head, turning from the cooling liquid comfort in front of him and stared at his daughter, stood behind the kitchen table. Her own cup was drained and lying, discarded, by her left elbow. There were marks and dents in that table, product of the time that Trisha's brother Jake had gotten loose with a hand drill once, long ago on a summer's day. He had been helping his father. Jake was always so helpful...

"It wasn't your fault,"

He reached for another Rich Tea biscuit. Like everything it did, he was careful; always aware of his hands shaking as he did so. Finally, he spoke:

"Does the Social know you're here?" He bit into the biscuit. It seemed to suck the moisture from his mouth as he did so. "They took you away after..." He swallowed, "After it happened. They wouldn't want to see you back here,"

She sighed, throwing her head back to show off the rose tattooed to her neck.

"I'm 18. They don't know or care now Dad,"

She sat down, avoiding his gaze, staring at the pile of grease covered plates on the worktop, the novelty penguin clock with its eyes moving from side to side and the last month's worth of newspapers jamming the back door closed. They sat in silence for a while, listening to the ticking of the clock. She was surprised it was still working.

"It wasn't your fault," she said again.

He took another bite from the biscuits. Police, social workers, judges: they had all listened to his arguments that it wasn't his fault. They had listened and made their own decision. Saying the same to his daughter would do him know good now.

"I was watching him," Trisha said.

"You were twelve!" There. He'd managed to condemn himself finally. His counsellor would be so proud.

"And still looking after both of you for a good few years before that,"

He laughed despite himself.

"How are you?" he said.

"Fantastic," she said, "Didn't you get the invite to my Nobel prize award?"

"They told me I wasn't allowed to contact you..."

"Do you think I cared what they say?" She stared straight at him now, "Is what the social say so important? I dropped out of college after my exam papers grew eyes and started trying to fly out the window. You can guess the rest,"

"Why did you come?" He sighed, put his head in his hands. She could see his collapsed veins standing out in his arms as he did so.

"Because I miss you," She said.

"There's too much, I can't..."

She threw her hands up, pushed her chair back.
"You're hopeless, you always were." She stood,
"I'll see myself out,"

She kicked a stone across the pavement ahead of
her as she walked home past red bricked house after
red bricked house, each with its overgrown garden
fenced off by thick black railings. Sad plastic toys lay in
long grass; mementoes of "Stop messing about and get
your tea," and "Sit there and stop bothering me". Terry
had been a better father than that but a failure in his
own way.

She'd hoped for so much more than that visit. He
was still the same as he always was, wrapped up in
himself, ineffectual, shiftless. The anger burned in her.

The sun was dipping now, the fields that separated
her old life from her new were covered in hazy mist in
the late light as she vaulted the fence, landing among
pathetic yellowish blades poking up from dry dirt
patches.

She pushed through the fields, heading out of the
town and down to a sheltered path. It lead her through
an overgrown river valley, past factories and old
industrial units long since become old shells and
skeletons cracked by ivy and tree roots that crept in
and out of the doors and windows. She left the city
behind, striding out into a twilight no man's land, a
true edge country.

A thin bridge lead across the river, nothing more
than a plank with an iron bar on each side to keep it in
place. On the far bank were only the grasping hands of
bare hawthorn and a phantom path on old maps. She
sat on the bank now, feeling the damp moss
underneath her and picking up the odd stone to chuck
at the bridge, trying to hit the metal and create the dull,
reverberating twang that she and Jake had achieved in
their childhood. The last time they had been here
together was that day, six years ago, when her father
had been preoccupied with his demons.

She felt the newcomer rather than saw him. There was a certainty to his presence that caused the hairs on the back of her neck to rise.

"You're still here," she said, not turning.

"I never left," It was a quiet voice, one that sounded like the leaves rustling against each other in the wind overhead.

"No one interferes with you here. They only interfere with the rest of us. Because of the mess that you left us with,"

"You blame me?"

She turned to face him. He was shorter than she remembered, but dressed as he always used to be, those old Reebok trousers and the black hoodie; the band's name on the back barely recognisable any more.

"I need to blame someone,"

He sat down next to her.

"Why? Things happen, people get injured. People get maimed. Sometimes they even die. If they didn't intend to, why do you blame them?"

"Because I'm angry you idiot! Because Dad blames himself and has wasted his life, cut himself off from me, his own daughter, because he blames himself, and it was all you. You and your silly games..."

A sigh, like the wind running through the trees and he shrugged.

"It doesn't matter to you does it?"

He listened to her and sat in silence for a minute or so, watching the dragonflies playing across the river. One disappeared in a set of ripples that radiated out towards the banks.

"What if," He said, "What if I had never shown you how to build that swing? What if you had stayed home, not just that day but every day, sat in your room, eating processed food out of plastic boxes and watching pathetic celebrities on a plastic screen?"

"What if we had?"

He shrugged.

"You know that,"

He pointed down the slope, to the edge of the water. It was still there, six years later. She knew it shouldn't be. There had been floods, other kids came down here all the time and it was good rope, too good to leave lying there.

Yet it was still there.

He scrambled down to the river, hardly seeming to sink into the sucking mud at all. He held the rope out to her.

"Tie it on,"

She shook her head.

"Go on, do it,"

She took the rope. It came back to her, the simple bow line, chuck it over a thick branch, slide the other end through, pull it tight.

There was another branch tied to the end. The swing was just as it was the last time Jake had showed it to her.

"Try it," he was behind her now, his breath warm against her neck, urging her on, pushing her, just as he had done that day. Images reached her mind again, the scream, the sickening crunch, her breath coming hot and rasping in her throat as she had run for help, choking back sobs, the blue lights as they played through the trees, the patch of mud, brown against the paramedics green knees and the feel of the space blanket, warm, as she stared numbly, disappearing into her own world.

She gripped the branch.

"No," She said, "I'm not a child any more, it's childish,"

His breath came against the other side of her face now, leaning against her other shoulder, his arm starting to encircle her.

"Exactly. You are your own person. You are free to do what you want. Go on, be free, stop being constrained by should and ought,"

It came in a rush, she jumped from the bank, the rope pulled tight. She hooked her legs around it as it soared out over the river, looping out into the empty air around her, screaming with delight, the years falling away and she went higher and higher, the swing taking her further and further. She came back to the bank as the trees creaked. Back out into the air, watching the shadows of the branches sway across the water.

Back in again, she breathed in, ready for the rush as she soared out again, listening to the creak of the trees, the splintering of the wood as, finally, again, the branch snapped.

Schadenfreude
Ollie Francis

The last time we argued, you hit me across the face full-on, in front of everybody. Maybe I deserved it. Who knows. I don't really think I'm the best person to judge these kind of things anyway. I'm too 'involved in the moment', as my old mum used to say. Even if I was trying to be honest about the whole thing, there would probably be something I would hold back; something I would keep even from myself, maybe, just to add that extra level of authenticity to my protests in the hope that this time — this one time — you would believe me.

But it was the look of your family that really got me. This was supposed to be it — our big weekend away together. A chance to heal all of those wounds from decades ago and play Happy Families late into the night; a last ditch attempt by your parents to stop everything from falling apart at the seams. Well, we put pay to that idea, didn't we my dear?

Oh god, it was glorious. There was the slap itself and the sting that quickly followed; sure, I didn't enjoy that bit very much. OK, so we once tried a bit of the old S&M in the bedroom, just to mix things up a little, but pain has never really been my sort of thing. I think we hold the record for the quickest ever use of the safe word. If it's not for everyone, then I am most definitely everyone. But it was the moment immediately after the attack that got me.

At first, just a second of silence. Just a second. No longer. A single tick of the clock. The birds stopped outside our window. The farmers in the fields stopped their tractors to get a better view. The squirrels in the garden stood up out of respect and waited for the world to draw breath again. If I'd known such a small action could have such a huge response, I think I would have done something to initiate it years ago. Utter, haunting, heavy, solid silence.

You see, in situations such as this, one often expects a reaction from the audience. We imagine it to be like that moment in the puppet theatre when Punch puts out a hit on Judy — the blow lands and the punters wait for the flurry to follow.

Are you not entertained?

But this was a bit different. For in this performance, it was neither Punch nor Judy who continued the action, but rather the watchers themselves in an awful parody of audience participation. Your mother spits at your father; your brother turns on your sister as they did when they were children; our brother-in-law leans in to defend her; your father winds up a hit on your mother before their son steps in to parry the strike; sister scratches at her husband for stopping her from fighting her own battles; mother screams and falls over grandchild; brother-in-law berates his mother-in-law for another example of irresponsibility; father has his shirt ripped open, pigeon chest exposed in a failed attempt at regaining his masculinity; all voices raise, all fingers pointing, and you and I stood in the centre of the kitchen, watching it all.

Schadenfreude. I guess that's what brought us together in the first place. It seems appropriate that it would have come to our rescue when our relationship was most in need of a little support. When everything

24

is falling down around your ears and all that you love seems to be coming to an end, it's sometimes good to take a moment and remember that somewhere, maybe closer than you might think, someone you know is going to be having a much worse time than you. I like to think we can take pleasure in that.

Stop, Look and Listen
Akeem Balogun

Stop.

My work colleagues tell me to stop smoking. They say it's detrimental to my health. "Do you want to see your future kids grow up?" they ask me. "Do you want us to stand next to you on the lunch break?"
I was pulled over by the police and told to stop speeding. "You could have killed someone," the officer said. "There's no way a child could have survived a hit at that speed."

A few of my friends and I were leaving a clothing store when security stopped me on suspicion that I had stolen something. They took me to one side, looked into my bag and checked the items against my receipt. They let me go once they saw all of it was on there.
My grandfather was quiet about the fact he needed financial help. I gave him an unexpected visit and found nothing in his fridge. I handed him some money and asked him why he was struggling. He said the government had introduced the Granny Tax to stop the growing deficit.

My girlfriend's flight to Turkey was stopped. There were fears of a terrorist attack. She told me "It's

27

probably nothing, just the counter terror police force looking for an excuse to use their weapons."
Common sense tells me that I should stop claiming benefits while working, but I can't when my bills keep going up but my income doesn't.

Look

I came across a street robbery. The attackers – or muggers – saw me and said "Stop looking. Carry on with your day."

Once, I went on a school geography trip. We were supposed to be looking at birds in the wild, but all I mostly saw were the fumes from the power plant nearby.

I got into a heated argument with my younger brother. He said he would make me see how much of an idiot I am and shoved a mirror in front of my face while I shouted at him. I looked at my twisted expression and fell silent.

The inlay booklet of the CD my neighbour gave me had the lyrics to the songs inside it. One of them read: "Take a look at the world and see what you can do to change it." It made me think for a while, and then I remembered I had thrown a couple coins into a bucket a man in a giraffe suit was carrying earlier.

and Listen

A friend I hadn't seen in a while told me he'd stopped listening to the news and that if he wanted to be depressed he'd just work more hours.
I rang the number behind a letter demanding I pay a small debt or "further action will be taken". The real price I had to pay was the twenty minutes of music-on-hold I had to listen to before somebody answered.

A work colleague told me he had never received good advice from anyone. What really bothered him was that most of the time the person offering it never took it themselves. I suggested he listened to one of God's and stopped committing adultery.

My niece came over for a visit. She moaned about how bad school was and how teachers always wanted her to stop looking at her phone in class. She asked me what I learned from listening to teachers back at school. I told her that they prepared me for a life and world full of instructions.

Fiona
Dave Attrill
(An Extract)

The brutal August rain beat down as she headed up the slope. June was not unused to it in Scotland, any more than her climb up this cruel backstreet each weekday. She was only envious that her old Yorkshire hometown had reportedly sizzled in seventy-eight degrees heat this last month. Trudging up to the pedestrian crossing, she let the Glasgow rush-hour rumble by before reaching the turn and the road she knew - one that had less trees than it could do with in this weather. Her workplace stood three doors short of the end, overlooking the M8. Trying to count the lampposts until she reached it made her look odd, but it took her all the way without the weather worrying her.

As she got to No6, she could see little light on inside the top floor windows. Someone was definitely still in - the front door to the tenement stood slightly open. Her employer usually did this just as she was expecting June to arrive: these old Victorian doors certainly knew how to stick. She took the tiled pathway one step at a time, remembering how deadly those tiles were in the wet.

Stepping in, out of the elements, the stairwell seemed just as uninviting. June was soon overcome by the acrid linger of overdue coal tar soap, or whatever they'd washed the tiles with all these years. Somehow it seemed wasted: today's early evening darkness denied them their shine. Noticing a light switch at her left, she thought 'stuff it'. Her safety up these slippery, worn-down stairs was more important than helping the place stay looking old or haunted.

June took the stairs a single one at a time, just as she had done with the path. She reached the third floor, where the door to flat 6B was at her immediate left, dark red and unwelcoming. Like back outside, there was little evidence anyone was at home today. No glow came from the crack round the letterbox.

She knocked politely.

"Hello. You there, duck?"

"I'm here." A small young voice shouted from deep within. "Wanna come right in? You know where to find him."

Making the most of her welcome, June twisted the doorknob clockwise and waltzed inside, taking off her coat. She shut the door behind herself, facing right down the hallway and its horrendous brown carpet. The rain-ravaged sky outside did not exactly make it look like summer within. The back bedroom already depended on daylight alone. Electricity across the apartment had lately been partly severed by Strathclyde Civil, due to previous unwanted visitors with syringes squatting the night, downstairs. She saw the flat becoming a ghost of the age-old Glaswegian slum it had grown from. As a second-generation Scot herself, she'd heard the stories of shoddy-to-non-existent lighting, of families sleeping in the cubby hole in their kitchen or lounge: no actual bedrooms existed in those days.

Sounds of a very young child bawling from his cot, drowned out her doldrums. June turned the handle down and dipped her head delicately through the door to see him.

"Boo..." She tried not to be too loud, just enough to turn him in his tears.

The small child was sitting upright against his pillow, wailing at her though the bars of his cot. She crept in gingerly, putting her bag down. Trying the light in hope of luck, it still didn't turn on. She left the door open, letting the light from the hallway help her cause. As it showed up the child in his small red-and-white onesie, she could see his face. The tears seemed to have subsided. June tried standing at the other end of the cot, as to abate her shadow. As she reached down to feel him, she found a moist patch on his trousers.

"Ooh...who's been having a little wazzy then?" The tot started crying once again.

"Cheer up, sunshine..." She encouraged him, although she still couldn't help think the conditions he slept in had something of a bearing on it "Come on, your auntie Junie will sort you out with clean undies." June scooped the infant carefully out of his cot and carried him along to the bathroom. The tot began to wail once more.

She placed him slowly onto the towel and made him comfortable before returning for a change of nappies.

"Hello..." she called to the other door, en route.

"Elaine? You alright in there?"

No reply came from his mother.

"Just gonna sort his undies out - the little monkey's messed them yet again, heh heh"

June looked round again towards a rude hall of silence then back at the baby. She headed into the bedroom to break out a fresh pair. On her way back across, she listened out for his mother but still received little answer. She was suddenly fetched back into the bathroom by the ascending stench. Placing the cleans on the side she removed the offending set from the child as fast as she could and folded them away into a Disposa-Bag, then felt round for the new ones: she already forgot where she'd left them. The door suddenly behind her suddenly opened with a tuneful creak.

Light from the hallway became blocked by a shadow June recognised.

"There you are…" she welcomed the figure in the doorway. "You've been a bit quiet since you got in. Difficult day, were it?"

The other woman didn't answer out loud. Remaining mute, she moved in across, straight up to the nanny.

"Ell?"

June turned round again, only to find her employer standing right behind. Looking face to face with her scornfully, the mother didn't yet speak.

"What's up, love?" June asked.

"I told you never to touch his cot. So what do you do?"

"The boy needed a change of…"
June didn't have time to finish as she was pinned against the chest of drawers behind her.

She found herself fighting for air as two sharp hands held a garotte-like grip on her throat, thrashing her head violently backwards into the wood.

"Don't worry, babe." the girl spoke aloud to the tot on the toilet, who could probably neither hear, nor understand "Your Auntie June's just hurt herself. Mummy will bring ye your keckies… few seconds." The young woman carried her boy into the bedroom and set him back gently into his bed. She winked at him before closing the door.

The novel 'FIONA', by D.W. Attrill, is available online at Amazon in Kindle and paperback.

Time to go home
Anna Simmons

I have always had a fascination with old things. Old houses, old objects, old people. I was born a middle-aged man, at least that's what my mother always said.

The more recent the change to the modern world, the more I seem to despise it and I greatly dislike the culture that the internet has brought so powerfully and unforgivably upo us.

The online world shows how vintage shops and antiques have sprung back into fashion, but people just want the clothes and the décor, they don't really want to return to that way of life. I think that's why I so much liked Mr Radley. He was in his sixties, so older anyway, but he had more than up-held a traditional way of life and, much like me, seemed to want to live in a different time entirely. He was always so well researched and came to the Emporium regularly to rummage through our three floors of musty and marvellous old items.

"Do you have any old dressing tables?" he asked one Saturday, having already selected a blue pair of heels and some fine lace gloves.

"There were plenty near to the doorway Mr Radley."

"I saw those," he said, taking out a striped handkerchief and wiping away the sweat that had gathered at the rim of his hat.

"I need a 1950s table, a white one if you've got any more. With roses on it preferably, although I can always paint those on."

He looked warm and worn from his search and the skin under his eyes was streaked with veins. I worried about him coming for such long periods of time to lift and shift through all our clothes and furniture. He looked tiny amongst the things he bought, but he always insisted on struggling with them alone around the shop and eventually back to his car. It was concerning too that he bought so many women's clothes, although I've always believed that what people get up to in their own home is entirely up to them. "I'll let you know first if we have any dressing tables that come in Mr Radley, you needn't worry about that."

A few months passed before he visited again. No white dressing tables of any kind had come in, but I had left him a message about a 1950s oak one that had recently arrived. Mr Radley seemed very agitated the day he came to see it and when he reached up to wipe his handkerchief under his hat, I noticed that there were also large swells of sweat under his armpits.

He inspected the table thoroughly but seemed pleased.

"Can you do the job of painting it white?" he asked me as he bent down to inspect the drawers.

"Well, yes, but why would you want to paint authentic solid oak?"

"Well it's been a long enough wait for a white one. This one will have to do."

As I wrote down the details of exactly what Mr Radley wanted (I'd asked for him to sign and pay before I began ruining that elegant old piece of wood) I noticed Mr Radley had begun to move from side to side on each foot. He was now perspiring so much from his ever-flowing forehead that a ball of sweat was fast making its way towards his bushy eyebrows.

"In a hurry, sir?" I asked as I handed him his receipt.

"Yes," he said, "I've had to lock her in the car." And then he rushed out of the Emporium in embarrassment or shame, quite clearly regretting what he had just divulged to me.

What Mr Radley had said concerned me, of course. But he seemed to me such a harmless man, that even though he had so clearly confessed he had someone shut in his car, I didn't call the police. The more I thought about it the more I believed that 'she' must have been some alter ego or something non-human like a pet or precious object, even a poor dead wife's ashes.

When I finally delivered the table to him three weeks later (it took me a while to make myself sand, paint and professionally ruin the damned thing) I was surprised to find that I was wrong and that the 'her' he had referred to was not a pile of grey embers, nor Mr Radley introducing himself as 'Mrs Radley' in pink lipstick and stockings, but a real-life woman. A revelation that actually worried me more.

"It will need to go upstairs" said Mr Radley, welcoming me into a small and delicately decorated living room. I was pleased to see the place was completely untouched by the horrors of modernity, without even a television or any magazines, something I had never quite been able to achieve in my own home. I would have stared for longer at the moss coloured furnishings and the stained wooden wireless that languished in the corner, but I was too interested in the real antique, his wife, who sat quietly sewing by the fireplace.

"Hello, one of Maurice's friends? Well do come in." I realised 'Maurice' was Mr Radley, he had never disclosed his first name to me. I introduced Mrs Radley to Roger, who had come from the Emporium to help me get the dressing table upstairs, but she never looked up from her sewing again and Mr Radley quickly clapped his hands and ushered us out to get going on the job.

It was a difficult task getting the great white beast up the stairs, especially with the mirror forming an extra hazard as it loomed above us, reflecting the rose papered walls and our rose tinged faces as we struggled on.

The bedroom we were directed to was as gorgeously time-trapped as the downstairs, with a white metal bed, in excellent condition and even an old bath tub propped in the corner. Disturbingly there were also China dolls and straw filled bears piously positioned around the room and on the bed.

"By the window, if you please", said Mr Radley. He looked very different without his hat on, somehow reminding me of a skinned rabbit.

When we returned downstairs Mrs Radley had set out a silver tea set, another 1950s masterpiece that I was pleased to behold. Roger soon made his excuses and left, he was an incredibly shy and unsociable man and I'd only given him a job at the Emporium after many visits from his mother, who would endlessly tell me how much he liked and how talented he was at tidying clothes.

"Where did he have to rush off to?" asked Mrs Radley, showing her creamy dentures in a smile.

"Back to work," I said, "he's a hard working man." Mrs Radley passed me a plate which was delightfully arranged with rich tea biscuits. As I took one she smiled again. "Works at the mills does he?"

"No," I said, "at my shop". Looking over at Mr Radley's widened eyes, looped by their unforgiving wrinkles and veins, I daren't tell Mrs Radley that the mills had been closed since before I was born.

"Greengrocers, is it?"

"No, furniture, clothes, antiques." I was about to mention the dressing table but Mr Radley's eyes told me not to.

"How lovely, Maurice, pour the tea and I'll get some more biscuits."

Mr Radley seemed afraid of the hot silver pot as he moved towards it but once he had hold of it he swiped it up so swiftly that he scarcely missed clonking me on the head.

"Empty" he announced and joined Mrs Radley in the kitchen. It was then that I noticed the sugar bowl and milk jug were completely empty too.

When they had finally sorted the tea it was obvious that Mr Radley did not really want me to stay much longer. As I gulped down my brew Mrs Radley continued to speak of the mills and then started talking about her mother and father who worked there, continuously referring to them as though they were still alive. Each word of this was like a stab wound to Mr Radley, who was increasingly melting into his chair as he watched us converse. When my cup was finally empty, I instantly made my excuses to leave.

"Mrs Radley, thank you for the lovely biscuits and tea, I would stay longer but I really must get back to my business now."

I began making my way out of the front door when, to my surprise, Mrs Radley came charging out with me, she was startlingly strong for such a small withered woman.

"I must go too, mother will be needing me!" Mr Radley looked achingly sad and rehearsed as he took his wife's arm and carefully dragged her in.

"You have to wait here for your mother", he tried to say cheerfully, and after some persuasion Mrs Radley returned to the house as I escaped down the drive.

I visited the Radley's again many times after that. I think Mr Radley was relieved that someone else was in on the game. It must have been a wearisome thing to play, for Mr Radley tried everything to convince his wife that this was her home, her childhood home if it had to be, to stop her always trying to go. Neither of us ever spoke about the dilemma, but it was raised regularly enough by the scratching of the chain lock on the door and the cheery "Goodbye" that introduced and concluded Mrs Radley's fantasy farewells.

Whether I was right or wrong I admired Mr Radley for what he was doing. He was creating a whole world for his wife and I knew that this was what all the things from the Emporium were really for. His wife described and spoke of her childhood house so often and in such detail that Mr Radley thought he knew exactly what he needed to make her feel at home again.

She liked the deep forest carpets and the dark wood wireless in the corner. She loved the China dolls that lived in her bedroom and she adored the dressing table, which her mother had decorated with painted pink roses.

Mr Radley did not visit the Emporium many more times after we had found the table and never bought anything else so big. He gathered a few other items; a perfume bottle, a hairbrush, a bag of assorted dress patterns. The perfume bottle had a dirty tinge to it, but Mr Radley said it would have to do. He seemed to be growing restless about something. He looked tired that day at the Emporium, as he shoved the green scent bottle into his bag, but then he always did look tired. He was trapped in a world that his wife was manically weaving back to life. But how could he unravel it when it was all that was keeping her happy and safe?

The next time I went to see the Radley's we had tea and biscuits from the silver service much the same and Mrs Radley forgot the hot water in the pot again. We spoke about the town and the mills and nice walks in the area. They both seemed quite happy somehow, although Mrs Radley still tried tried to come with me again as I left. As Mr Radley soothed his wife back into the house he unexpectedly passed me a letter. "I'm not good with words," he said. "And I just wanted to show my gratitude to you."

I read the letter as soon as I got back to the shop. It was beautifully written, although, typically of Mr Radley, it was more polite than heartfelt. He thanked me for helping him find the things he needed during all the times he had visited the shop and for coming to see them at their home, when it was something I was never obliged to do. He said that he was grateful for my efforts finding all the things they needed and that it was a shame that things hadn't worked out.

I'm sad to say that Mr and Mrs Radley left my life soon after that. They were found in the upstairs bedroom, entwined in strangled up sheets and both fully clothed. He had left a list of all the things he had bought at the shop, saying he wanted them returned to me for free.

It was difficult to go and collect all the items he had spent so long putting together. But the house felt empty, the most important things had gone. I think that Mr Radley just didn't want her to be afraid anymore. I think he knew that it was time to go home.

The Source of Eternal Youth
Sam Sharp

1899

Excitement springs through the scientific world as the elusive elixir to eternal youth has been found. Its source: squirrel testicles.

Doctor Horace Emmett, renowned physician, this week revealed to an eager crowd at the Biology Society of Magdalene College, Cambridge, his findings that red squirrel testicles can rejuvenate the self by decades.[1]

"Why, I feel thirty years younger," the 79 years old Dr. Emmett claimed.[2]

In answer to accusations of cruelty towards the red rodents Dr. Emmett produced "Alfie", his pet squirrel.[3] The doctor explained that even *sans gonad* the creatures can enjoy a meaningful life. Alfie the squirrel appeared agitated by the crowd's fascination and nibbled on an acorn.

---

[1]. Doctor Horace Emmett did indeed reveal these findings.
[2]. Dr. Emmett claimed this, though whether feeling 49 years old could be described as "youthful" is debatable.
[3]. Dr. Emmett may or may not have had a pet squirrel called Alfie. He probably didn't.

"But, Sir!" Came the cry of a young man from the audience. "Do you have to remove your own tallywags[4]?"

"My lad," replied Dr. Emmett, "I can assure you my tallywags have gone nowhere!" He then winked while the audience tittered.

The doctor continued by explaining that the squirrel testicles are ground up and the resulting pulp injected into oneself.

As well as bringing about youth, Dr. Emmett claimed further still that the pulp of red squirrel testicles increases virility.

"Without fail," the doctor assured, "I can visit my wife once a day."[5]

Dr. Emmett's wife did not attend the talk and was therefore unable to verify the veracity of the virility claim.

Still, without doubt this is a momentous landmark in the field of medical science.

1899 cont.

Two months ago, Doctor Horace Emmett announced his supposed discovery of eternal youth by means of self-injecting the pulp of red squirrel testicles. Since, Mrs. Emmett has left the doctor for a younger man[6], and now we must sadly tell of Doctor Horace Emmett's death from cerebral haemorrhage.[7]

Dr. Emmett's colleges inform us that the testicles of red squirrels are no longer revered as a source of eternal youth.

In addition, anyone wishing to foster a castrated red squirrel may inquire to the Biology Society of Magdalene College, Cambridge. Ask after Alfie.

---

[4]. "tallywags" was Victorian slang for "testicles." Other Victorian slang for testicles included "trinkets" and "twiddle-diddles".
[5]. Another claim made in favour of squirrel testicles.
[6]. One wonders if the younger man not injecting himself with squirrel testicle pulp had something to do with it.
[7]. Sadly, this is how Dr. Emmett met his end.

Home help
Martyn Shenton

I'm only eighty-three, you know. They call me old. I'm not old. Old's them who haven't got much use left. I'll tell you now, I can do anything I ever could, with a bit of concentration. They treat old like it's a number, but I think it's something that's done to you. I'm not old; they make me old by keeping me cooped up here and not letting me do owt for myself. They think I don't see it.

"Sorry, but we can't keep going on like this. You need to consider your options," the hospital says. Well, they might not be able to keep going on but I think I can keep going on just fine, thank you. I tell them, I've still got all my faculties. They tell me they keep finding me in funny places. I think it's a ploy to get me off to the home. Still, it's not up to me anymore, is it? So, I have a girl come to clean up and tend after me. I forget her name.

She's due any minute now, I think. She normally makes an appearance come the early afternoon. Too late to make me dinner and too early to make me tea, but just the right time to sit me on the lavatory and expect me to make my movements on cue. I tell her

49

though, I'm not too old to wipe. That's for them fresh of this world or them soon to leave it. Bernie wouldn't have stood for any of this, God rest his soul.

Oh, he was a right one my Bern was. We met at Silk's Cutlers when we were both apprenticing. He was a shaper and I was a finisher. He'd cut the steel down to what they needed, knives, spoons and the like, then put them in a press for shaping. When they got to me I had to polish them up good for selling. Bern was the best they had; never had a miss-cut in all his working days, or so he claimed. Me though, well, I think I kept my job because Mr Silk had a bit of a thing for me.

The night we met was the night of the work's do. Mr Silk had had a few champagnes and was getting a bit too close on the dancefloor. Hands all over, you know. Well, you didn't say anything back then, did you? But Bern, he comes marching right over and tells Mr Silk to go sit down. The whole room went quiet just waiting to see what would happen to this seventeen year old lad. Would you believe it, the old todger in the suit just walks off with his tail between his legs? Bern looks at me, winks, then goes straight back to dancing with Nancy Woodruff. It was me that he walked home though.

I've still got a picture from that night on my wall. It's all faded now and there's dust in the frame's edges. I'd love to give it a good clean, Bernie would have liked that. But, well, it's high up you see. I do wish I could reach it. I'd ask her that comes round but she'd only huff about it. I've got loads of photos. Me and Bern at work. Me and Bern at the wedding. Me and Bern at the beach. Me and Bern with that kiddie at the park. Loads of other people too, but it's hard to keep track of who's who. You know what it's like.

Sixty two years to the day we were together and sixty one to the day we were married. April 15th. It'll be the day I depart too, I'm sure of it. In all that time we were wed we didn't have a single day apart, Bern wouldn't have had it. Well, not til near the end, but that wasn't his fault.

It wasn't.

He was a proud man, my Bern. Proud at work and proud at home. He wasn't one of them that came back and stuck their feet up; expecting me to bluster around, cleaning and putting tea on the table. I'm not saying it was all smiles, I don't trust them that say owt ever is, but we had a lot more good than bad and you can't ask for better than that.

You know, our garden won prizes thanks to my Bern. All the time we were going with each other he was putting a bit away from his earnings each week and when we tied the knot he bought this place for us straight off. From the start, he put himself into that garden. I'll tell you what, there wasn't a day in all those sixty-odd years he didn't keep working on it either.

That was our special space that garden was. We'd sit out there with a blanket and jam sandwiches and have a picnic in the summertime. Bern said that made us right posh. And I don't mind saying, there were a couple of harder times where Bern's veg patch stopped us from going hungry too. The best bits though were the parties. We'd have people round, neighbours I think, or maybe folk from the church. It doesn't matter. Anyway, everyone would bring a bit to eat and we'd spend the day watching the kiddies play round the tree at the bottom.

Nowadays it's lucky if I get let out at all. Course, madam never bothers to so much as trim the hedge. It's so overgrown it looks common. A proper sad affair. The greenhouse is all smashed up and I dread to think what the local cats have left in the veg garden. I wish I could tell Bern what she's like.

Well, there's no point in mithering about it, is there?

It all properly went downhill after the trip to Cleethorpes. The girl who comes round and her fella, they asked me where I wanted to go out for a treat, like. Well, me and Bernie, that was our special place, you see. So, I asked if I could go and sit by the boating lake like we used to when we were courting.

Course, it wasn't really a treat for me, was it? I clocked that from the start. When you want to treat someone, you do something for them don't you? You don't do something for yourself and pretend it's for them. I knew what their game was as soon as they bundled me in to the back of the car. They sat me between them two kiddies and put the beach bag on my knee. The boating lake's nowhere near the beach.

As soon as we got there the kiddies were all "can we do this?" and "can we do that?" I didn't have much say in the matter, of course. They were spoiled rotten them two. Me, on the other hand? Well they thought they could keep me happy with a bench and a cheap ice-lolly. With my teeth? It was like jamming a nail an inch into my gums.

"Don't worry, we'll get to the lake in a bit." They said. Yeah, I thought. Right after none of the ducks want feeding and the boats are tethered for the night. "Just have to let the kids do this that and the other first, don't we?" Bern would have put them right in their place. It's not right not keeping promises. He didn't like a liar.

I can still get up with my stick when I need to. So, when they were preoccupied I got going. I got myself in a taxi and asked him to drop me by the lake. Nice lad. Foreign feller, but you could understand him alright. He dropped my off and offered to walk me up the path, but I paid him on his way. Only thing is, I got a bit confused then and the next thing I know it's gotten dark and cold and I can't see the park anymore and there's blue lights and police and everyone's shouting and I just want to go home to be with my Bern.

Now, I know what you're thinking, and you can cut it right out. When you've seen as many parks as I have, they all start to look the same after a while. I thought, just for a second, I was back in the park at home. It doesn't mean a thing.

So now I'm lumped with Miss High-and-Mighty trying to pry on my unmentionables every day. Do they take any notice that I don't want her here? Do they eckers like. She's a right grumpy so-and-so that one; a face like a smacked arse. She walks about like she's doing me a favour, or like the world owes her one. I tell you now, my Bernie won't stand for this when he gets back.

Where is he? He's never late back. I've checked the garden and he's not out there. I bet he's out fishing again. He'll stink the place right out when he gets in. It takes an age to scrub the smell of trout out of his clothes when he's had a good day. No matter how many times I ask him to take his gear off outdoors. It's not right him not being here. I want him here. I want him with me.

Here she is now, look. Just comes waltzing in like she owns the place. Straight in without even asking. She comes round all the time you know, uninvited.

"Have you had a nice day?"

"Never you mind, have I had a nice day. You need to call the police."

"Oh, not today, I don't have the energy."

"Bernie's missing."

"No, he's not."

"I haven't seen him since... Since..."

"Shall I make you a drink?"

"A drink? No! I want you to get the police. Why don't you understand?"

Why doesn't she understand?

She's at it again, eying up my pictures. I've seen her doing it before; I think she's after the frames. Me and Bern, we always get proper frames you see, the ones that cost a bit more but you know are going to last.

"Look, why don't we have a look for him; me and you together, eh? Maybe that will help?"

She doesn't understand how urgent this is.

"No, we bloody well can't you useless cow! My husband should have been back... Well... He should be here."

She looks at me for a second, right at me and when she does it comes to me, her name is Mary; it comes to me from nowhere.

Mary.

I've always liked that name.

Then she does it again; she looks up at the photos on my wall. I bet she can't wait to get me out of here so she can sell off the lot. I know what these help types are like. Vermin. The bloody lot of them are on the take. Out for what they can get. They don't give two hoots about people like me, people like my Bern.

Oh Bern.

Where are you?

I see her looking at me.

"Mum, come on. Let's get you up to bed."

Mary.

Bless her, she must be confused.

Burn
Ollie Francis

The chair was her mother's; the arms worn smooth by worry and long summer evenings. She leans back, feels the wood embrace her.

This is what she took from the house. Everything else was left, all of it reminders of moments she preferred to forget. But she was always going to save the chair. There was something about its contradiction that consoled her. It was hard and unpadded, yet comfortable; old and woodwormed, yet sturdy beyond anything Ikea would ever offer her.

Taking it from the house was probably the biggest task. Its weight had meant she had dragged it across the parquet flooring of the kitchen, leaving unsightly gouge marks across its surface. Her mother would have hated that, if she had lived. Understandably, she supposed. But that hardly mattered now.

She pulled her feet beneath her, now fully curled onto the seat of the chair. The fire was getting hot.

There had been something about their last argument. It had a sort of finality to it. There was a moment when she just recognised (preternaturally?) that it was over. All those years of bickering and this would be their last. There would be a part of her that would miss it.

But times move on, she told herself. What would be coming next would be something entirely new, she understood that. It scared her a little, but she understood it. It was a little like the matchbox in her hands — she knew what was in there, but the details, the exact number, was hidden to her for now. She would have to open it up again to find out.

She lay her head against the tall back of the chair, feeling the air crackle around her. She had to shut her eyes to the heat of the flames now. Maybe she should have moved the chair to the pavement; she worried that her weight would sink it into the damp ground of the early morning grass. But it had been so heavy to drag, even just to the front lawn.

She nestled herself further into the wood of the chair, letting herself drift into its fibres. She was so tired now, so very, very tired. She would have slept, but the fire was so very beautiful and it would have been a such a shame to have missed it.

Fish and Chips
Leanne Williams

Aggie missed the feeling of dread that used to slink in to the corners of her Sunday evenings. The way that Monday quivered at the edge of her vision, promising the inevitability of the fluorescent lights of the office and the stench of the lunchroom fridge. When she reached her sixties she had actually started noting the time left in the wall calendar, crossing off each day with a triumphant pink highlighter, much to Harold's amusement. She would be the first past the post, breaking out into pension-padded freedom; but now that the dream had manifested into reality she found herself adrift. Her Sundays sloped off into her Mondays without ceremony and she had little else to do but watch the street outside gradually empty each morning.

Harold later joined her, initially red cheeked and glowing with promise. But he soon found himself at her side, doing little else but contemplating the Tescos delivery van that trundled to number 23.

"Must have a baby elephant in there." He said one morning, propping his mug of tea on his belly.

"Mm?"

"Well, it's the third time she's had the van here this week." he laughed and flinched away from the inevitable spill.

"Always bloody round." he fanned at his cardigan. "How big can one woman's fridge be?"

Aggie stood up, flicking a napkin up from the table and tossing it to him. "What on earth are you talking about? He comes 'round every Wednesday, when she's at home with the kiddies."

Harold froze mid-dab and stared at her.

"Every-? Don't be daft, woman."

"Every Wednesday." she insisted. "Just Wednesdays."

Harold went rather quiet after that.

That Friday Aggie was wrenched awake by something she hadn't heard in months: the blaring alarm clock. She shrieked, groping out only to find Harry's hand already pressed down on it. He stood over the bed, a boyish grin on his face and her favourite mug in his hand.

"Morning Mrs. Are you up then?" He passed her the tea and pecked her on the cheek. "Busy day ahead."

It wasn't long before she was sat beside him in the car, eased a little by caffeine and the promise of the thermos in the boot. He de-steamed the windscreen with a bobbing impatience that she hadn't seen since their wedding. Harold had been thin as a whippet back then, his suit rumpled, stood at the end of the church with that willing smile on his face as if he could convince her father to scoop her over his shoulder and run down the aisle with her to hurry things up a bit. She touched his hand.

"Harry, what on earth's gotten into you?"

"We're getting out of here, all right? Do you remember before the kids were born, that little restaurant across in the next town? Every Friday like clockwork we'd be there, you with your lipstick on." He smiled at the memory and shifted the car into gear.

"Well, here we are. The kids have left home, what's stopping us?"

Aggie smiled at the memory of the old tiny car and Harold's figure bunched up in it, all wonky tie and elbows. She had loved to watch him drive and he was an eager chauffeur. She'd never driven again after that: he liked to treat her like royalty back then. Now the roads seemed so fast and so busy she was glad of him. Well, she was always glad of him really. When it came down to it.

"I remember" she murmured. "But we can't stretch to the Piccolo's every week anymore."

Harold sighed. "I know that, love, I wasn't about to. Fish and chips then. All the ones round here are nothing but scraps. Let's go to the next town and find a new one. Come on, my treat. Something to pass the bloody time! I feel like a goldfish stuck in its bowl in that house."

Aggie giggled. "I told you; take up gardening like the Wilsons if you're bored."

"I've as much luck with petunias as you have with a crochet hook." Harold smirked.

Aggie rolled her eyes, but shifted closer to lean on his shoulder. A warmth of nostalgia eased into her bones.

"All right then. Haddock before horticulture."

It took them a while to find the place. Aggie had always used the bright theatre house as a landmark, but it had long gone. She had a vague recollection of a car park opposite, but now a Sainsbury's seemed to wrap around half the street.

"There was always one in the city centre?" She suggested, though was uneasy about how they might find it again. The arrangement of the buildings was all off and she had never had much of an eye for the logic of the roads.

"Ah, they only cater for the kids going clubbing. You could batter pencil shavings and they'd eat it."

Harold chuckled. "Residential's where it's at. Give me a minute, love."

Eventually they weaved down to a terraced street, wedging themselves between the rows of cars. Aggie pressed her nose to the glass of the passenger window, eyeing the wing mirror as if will alone could keep them intact. Sure enough, pushed next to a squat Methodist church was the glowing frontage of "*Cod-rophenia*".

"Easy as that." Harold said after a rather lengthy parallel park. They heaved themselves out and Aggie stood uncertainly at the entrance. Harold soon linked up arms with her and they stepped in to the warmth of hot fat and the tang of vinegar in the air. As they ordered - two fat cods, mushy peas and enough chips to feed an army -Aggie smiled and squeezed his arm, feeling her bravery seep in as surely as his warmth did with hers.

"Come on, we'll eat it outside." She decided with a spark of daring.

"Not in the car?" He looked doubtful.

"Outside." She insisted. "Come now, if this is going to be an authentic adventure we have to eat it outside on our laps, like with the kids down at Bridlington. The cold makes it taste better and besides, you need the exercise."

They stepped outside, holding the warm newspaper to their chests. Aggie retrieved the thermos from the boot and was away, pulling Harold with her towards the high street.

The fish and chips steamed gently in the cold air. Harold reached over to steal a chip and she returned the favour, heaping mushy peas into her prize.

"Do you reckon our restaurant is still there?" She asked.

"It was only a little place." Harold shrugged.

"Probably a McDonald's now. Everything else is."

"Not Piccolo's." Aggie insisted.

Certain things can't change when so much history is loaded within them, she was sure. Her old school still stood, the old political parties blinked in and out with the same infuriating routines as ever. Even the church where Harold had grinned at her was still there - unimpressive in sandstone and decorated with the same damned leaflets that had been there since the kids were, well, kids.

She knew that Piccolo's was maybe five minutes' drive down the road and then veered left around a sharp turn, because Harold used to have a habit of taking it too quickly and giving one of those laughs that he thought was bravado but was quite clearly panic. As they walked, delicately picking at the flakes of cod, he didn't make any move to correct her progress and fell neatly into step. She was certain that she was on the right route. Sure enough, she soon recognised a pebble-dashed house that had always had overgrown privets. They were clipped more neatly now and the gate had been replaced. Piccolo's was opposite.

At least, it used to be.

Piccolo's had been an unusually squat and wide building, wedged where the terraces broke apart. But the old floor length windows with the half curtains were now plastered in an awkward attempt at creating a residential frontage. The door, once adorably in the middle, had been wrenched off to one side. A bare stud-scarred wall was all that was left of the distinctive sign. The window glowed with cool white light behind full length curtains, flickering with the silent hidden images of the television inside.

Harold sighed, reaching out for the small of her back. She shrugged him off and made a play of focusing on stabbing at her chips, but her eyes were fixed forward.

No. Of course it wasn't there.

"It has been a while." Harold said softly when it was clear that Aggie wouldn't speak first. He didn't quite have the resolve to touch at her arm again in case she snapped at him. "Do you want to sit down here and finish up?"

"No." Aggie said. She saw movement behind the curtains, a faint shadow of disturbance as if the person inside could sense their loitering. She couldn't stand a face appearing territorially at the window and turned away before it had the chance. "Let's go back to the car, alright?"

Harold gave a thin smile and nodded, walking close to her. Aggie seemed to have lost interest in her chips. When they reached a bin he gently scooped them up with his own and tossed them aside.

They squeezed into the car and he turned the heating up full blast, waiting for the windscreen to unfog. Aggie fussed about putting the thermos into the footwell. He wanted to give her leg a squeeze in assurance but he knew it wouldn't help. She'd had the same look in her eyes when Jake had announced that he was moving down to London for work. Or when the teenage arguments with Sam had cut that little bit too deep. Harold felt old.

It wasn't until they were halfway home that he chirped up again, determined to coax her out of her mood.

"Well the chips were a bit pale, but I'd say they were quite decent, eh?" he suggested, carefully planting his lure.

"Mm. Nice fish. Not too fishy." She agreed, stretching in her seat a little.

"Fishy? It's fish."

"You know. They can be *too* fishy." she insisted. "My mother always said that if you fish *tastes* like fish then it'll be off. Old."

"Your mother never had salmon." Harold scoffed and was relieved when Aggie cracked a smile.

"Salmon shouldn't be too fishy either." she tutted. "The stuff in tins doesn't count."

"Rubbish!"

"I'm telling you; good fish and chips should taste clean. That one did."

"It did." he agreed. "We'll have to do another taste test. With a good fish and chip shop. High quality and all that. The sort with stars in the window. Here, how about that one in Whitby? Magpie's or whatever it's called."

"Whitby? Who's going to go all the way out to Whitby just for fish and chips?"

"Whitby is *made* for fish and chips. There's no other point to the place."

The next week it was no weather for Whitby, with pelting rain and with the cold still biting in the wind. But the thermos was bundled into the boot once more and Harold had found out a CD from a few Christmases back so there were no excuses. The drive took far longer than planned, with several stops for him to stretch out his stiff knees and for Aggie to hurry to the ladies', but soon enough they were in the wilds of Dracula country. Their prizes were wrapped in fancy cardboard containers against the circling seagulls. As they nestled under the pavilion Aggie declared them the best fish and chips that she had ever had. Harold sniffed.

"You have to admit that the mushy peas are a disappointment though." he observed, with the measured tone of a barrister weighing his case

"No one", Aggie snorted, "buys fish and chips for the *peas*".

Harold, of course, was adamant. He often was. Mushy peas were the crescendo to a grand culinary orchestra and if only Aggie tasted them properly she would understand. In his opinion he had never tasted mushy peas like those at Blackpool when he was a boy, in a shop that was near the big tower. They were greener than grass.

Well, of course they had to go.

It was that way week after week, chasing the lure of some perfect meal. Aggie had been nervous about the extra length of the drive that Blackpool would entail, but in the end what else had they to do? When the alarm buzzed them awake she felt a thrill of purpose and they eagerly competed with the commuters for road space.

They were in Inverness when it happened.
They put together for a hotel room in this, their first stay in a 'new country'. The journey had been almost intolerably long but they had broken it up how they could with roadside cafes and frothy coffees. Harold had been wheezing and Aggie had been steadily plying him with lozenges as he drove to clear up his airways, occasionally taking one for herself as a 'preventative measure'. Harold had teased her and it had passed a while at least.

The hotel itself was modest, with brown flocked carpets that reminded Aggie of visits to her Aunt back when she was younger. Harold had left her in charge of collecting the hotel keys and hurried back to the boot to take out the night bags.

She had stood at the desk making small talk with the receptionist with the thermos tucked under her arm.

She stood and paid the deposit.

She stood as the small talk petered out.

She stood and pretended to be interested in the painting above the receptionist's head.

Harold did not come back.

Minutes later, when she was bunched up on a chair behind the desk of that same reception, she found herself shell shocked by how silent it had been. She expected a cry, some noise, even a thud. He had never weathered so much as a headache without dramatic complaint in his life. But there had been nothing at all. Harold had simply not come back.

A week later, Harold's car still stood in the driveway.
Like a brick. At the funeral she sat in the front row,
feeling everyone's eyes on her. Sam was sobbing into
her coat sleeve, wiping her nose on it like she had
when she was an infant. Jake, crumpled from the train
ride, held Sam's hand and squared his jaw against the
whole thing like he had carried them all from the start.
Aggie couldn't tether herself. The coffin was laid out
on the table like some gaudy display and the thing
inside was nothing but cold meat. A *thing*. Not Harold.
She wanted to burn it and have done with it.
The coffin was cavorted around like it ought to be
fawned over and there was suitable performance from
the audience when the curtain went around it and it
disappeared. Aggie wanted to make a noise: a cry
perhaps, but she wasn't sure that it was in the way that
she was supposed to. She was afraid that if she let it
out the gagging grief would come out as a snarl.
She was very still. The event, like all others, passed
without incidence.

The car was still there in the driveway when she
came home.

The house was empty and quiet. Aggie hadn't
realised how much noise Harold made, whether it was
the perpetual boil of the kettle, or the soft occasionally
limping footfalls. A cough or a murmur or even, god
help us, a sneaky bout of flatulence that he thought he
had gotten away with. There was no buzz of the TV or
a rattle of magazines. It was as if the sound and even
the colour were bleaching away from the place.
When she thought that the neighbours were out, she
would creep out and open up the car and slide into the
driver's side. She could still breathe him in. Only,
sometimes her from number 26 would put her bins out
so Aggie had to make a break for it back to the house
before she saw how red her eyes were.

Over the weeks they sifted through his clothes and packed up in boxes his razor and cufflinks and the shapeless cardigans and the countless magazines on model trains that he had never built. Jake had gone 'home' to London with Harold's pocket watch and Sam had sulked until Aggie appeased her with Harold's wedding ring.

On the seventh Friday Sam was around to show her how to trim the privet back ready for the spring and how to change the fuel in the lawnmower. When they sat in the living room with their hands wrapped around cups of tea Aggie saw the way Sam eyed the car when she thought she wasn't looking.

"Did you find out how much the insurance costs on that, mum?" Sam eventually asked. Aggie's heart seized.

"Around £750 a year, I think." She guessed, keeping her voice level.

"That much? Jesus mum, it's a money pit for you. And think of the maintenance."

"Well he had that ding back in September. You know what they're like."

Sam inhaled and Aggie stood up, cutting her off by making a move for the teapot.

"It'll go down in enough time." Aggie pointed out. Insurance had very much been Harold's domain, but she was sure that's how it worked.

"No it won't mum, not if no-one's driving it." Aggie could see her mentally digging in the trenches. "You ought to be rid of it. It'll be a weight off your mind."

"I'm driving it." Aggie said, too quickly. She heard Sam's breath catch as her daughter tripped over that notion and sought a change of approach. Aggie focused very hard on pouring the tea.

"You? Mum, you cannot lie to the insurance people; they will notice no one is driving it. Besides, it will rot just sat there and all the while you're paying tax and more." The slow measured tone Sam spoke in irritated her, she had developed that tone before she had even hit puberty, as if by drawing out each syllable it might permeate through her mother's thick skull.

"I'm driving it." Aggie insisted. "I have a licence, don't I?"

"Look." Sam sighed and shifted in her seat. "I know that it was dad's but, well it's really too much responsibility. It's not like you'd have anywhere to go anyway, we'll get you a bus pass and Tesco can make deliveries-"

"I'm off to Brighton next week." Aggie snapped, far louder than she'd meant to.

The plan had not entered her head before she had said it, she had just grasped for the first seaside town that she could think of. But once it took hold she found it harder and harder to not turn the idea over in her mind. It *had* been on their list, and Friday was coming up. Why not? Her heart hammered and she focused on drinking her tea to calm her, tuning out Sam's protests. Friday.

That evening Aggie slipped out to the car. The gearstick glared up at her, the blocky grid of numbers like teeth. She grimaced. Just like riding a bicycle, she told herself. Only, this one had a growling engine and enough bulk to flatten anyone stupid enough to get within a mile of her when she was behind the wheel. She tried to visualise herself as a young woman again back when the roads were near empty and she only had to worry about running over the local newspaper delivery boy. Back when licences were really just formalities.

But so much had changed since then. Lifetimes had risen up and faded away.

She found herself gripping the steering wheel until her knuckles were white. She released it and leant back, taking a moment to centre herself and breathe in Harold's scent. After a moment, she flexed her legs, balancing clutch and accelerator, easing her way in. It was like her sewing machine, she remembered. Too much and the fabric would be chewed up in the jaws of it, but if you hit that sweet spot you were away, as smooth as silk. She tried not to let any thoughts enter her head as she switched on the ignition. She flexed on the pedals again and pushed the car into gear. She could do this.

As it was, Aggie bunny-hopped the car down the street before it stalled with a crack at number 34. Her face was hot, and with some fumbling he managed to get it going again. Her heart thudded so hard that she could feel it in her throat, but it brought a sort of giddy adrenaline. She could imagine Harold laughing at her - - "dozy cow!" - and she found herself laughing too. She was laughing when she completed her circuit of the cul de sac and parked it at an angle on the drive.

The next time she headed out, she hadn't thought of a destination, it was enough just to be moving at all. When no disaster struck she then gently rumbled the car out onto the main road, shifting in her seat and readying her instincts as she pulled it up to thirty miles per hour. The main road was wider and she realised that really she could go anywhere she liked. She settled for following the route out to the supermarket, chewing on her lip as she navigated the local roundabout and emerged on the other side unmolested. The car seemed tamed under her but she could imagine how she looked: this doddery old woman peeking over the wheel and counting each roundabout exit aloud. When she arrived at the supermarket, car between the lines with no pedestrians caught on her bumper, she let out the cheer that had been building in her chest since she set off.

She could practically see Harold with that mocking little fanfare but with that warmth in his eyes that she knew meant he was chuffed to bits. She'd seen it the first time that she managed to produce a pie without the crust burning. She'd used it on him the first time he'd learnt to feed Sam without spilling half the food all over the poor mite.

"I expect you're pleased with yourself are you?" She would snark, and he'd give her a bear hug that she'd be wriggling away from until they relented into giggles. She felt the lump in her throat rise even as the smile was still on her face and she leant her head back to stare up at the carpeted ceiling of the car. It eased, as it always did if she stayed very still and didn't look the feeling in the eye. After a moment she squeezed her eyes shut and gave a little bark of a laugh.

"Oh good grief, Harry. I've got to get back home as well don't I?"

On Friday Aggie set her alarm. She packed the thermos, stashing it carefully in the footwell with her handbag pushed against it to prop it up and the map wedged underneath it. She felt giddy and unsteady, the adrenaline of terrifying reality and the excitement of possibility swirling around in her until her nerves buzzed with it. When she climbed into the driver's side and breathed in Harold's scent she found that her hands stopped shaking, though the smell was fainter every day.

"Buckle in then." She murmured. "I'll show you what mushy peas should taste like."

Pick N Mix
Akeem Balogun

Charming, cheeky and unpredictable: three words that described my father's nature more than it did his personality.

"I used to be careless," he told me once when we were sat in the living room.

I looked at him. "So? You turned out fine. Didn't you?" He laughed and told me the man sitting next to me wasn't all his doing, that years of mistakes and dozens of other people played a part too.

"My life was a pick 'n' mix box," he said, "and it wasn't all sweet." He looked into the corner of the room smiling at something I couldn't see.

"What do you mean?" I said.

"What? Oh yeah, nothing really. I used to be a bit of nuisance, that's all." He stood up stretching. "But not anymore."

I looked up at him. I wanted to ask him to tell me more, but I didn't. Instead, I nodded, and he erupted into laughter.

"You don't believe me do you?"

I stuttered but didn't manage to say anything.

"I didn't learn a thing," he said. "If I had, I never would've got married, and I never would've had children."

He chuckled, and I watched as he walked out of the room sniggering to himself.

Kev the Capitalist's Nightmare
Tim Ingham-Dempster

"... and your three o'clock's in room two, called Kev and I don't really know much about him apart from he rang when I was off and somehow wrangled a meeting." Sharon finished going through Mike's schedule for the afternoon as Mike nonchalantly shifted his weight so that he could get a better view of the man waiting patiently in the room across the hall. There was something awfully familiar about him causing a thought he couldn't quite place to jump up and down in the back of Mike's head. "But before that Daniels wants to see you, didn't say why."

"Oh great, guess I'll go see what that's all about then. Thanks Sharon, see you." Mike replied.

Mike stood still, breathed in, held it, exhaled a long breath through puffed out cheeks and knocked on the solid mahogany panelled door.

"Come in."

Mike squared his shoulders, opened the door and walked into the office behind with every ounce of the confidence he didn't feel.

"Ah Mike, take a seat" said Daniels with a warm smile, gesturing to one of the facing couches in front of his desk as he stood. Mike watched Daniels as he

79

strode over to the other couch and sat down. Perfectly slicked back black hair with just a hint of distinguished grey, crisp white cuffs exactly a half-inch below the sleeves of his freshly pressed navy blue suit, links showing a flash of gold and just visible a chunky steel wristwatch. Mike unconsciously flattened a crease on his own sleeve.

"So, how long have you been with us now?" asked Daniels

"About 18 months." Replied Mike with a puzzled frown.

"Really, that long? Doesn't the time just fly these days? And in total you've been in this business for about ten years yes?"

"Yes, that's right." Mike supplied.

"And how are you finding it here, do you enjoy working for us?"

"Yes thanks, no complaints so far."

"Ah, well, that makes this next part a bit trickier." Daniels glanced away and then looked back at Mike. "I'm afraid it's not going to work out for you here."

Mike leaned forwards as his stomach contracted into a ball of lead, he caught the arm of the sofa to steady himself and drew a few slow, deliberate breaths before replying through gritted teeth. "I see, can I ask why? Are you unhappy with my numbers?"

"No no, nothing like that, you've been an exemplary employee and your reference *should* reflect that, we'll do all we can to help you secure a position somewhere else. It's more of an, ah, personality issue." Daniels smile stayed on his face but it no longer reached his eyes.

"Thanks … err … can I ask what it is about my personality? Has someone complained?" Mike's head was spinning and he swallowed hard to keep down the bile building in his stomach.

"Not at all, in fact you're an exceptionally agreeable young man, it's just a sort-of, ah, feeling type thing, you don't quite fit. Can't really put our finger

on it but it just won't work out, I'm sorry." Daniels
gave him a fatherly smile and pat on the shoulder
before going on "Now ordinarily we would have
security escort someone out immediately, just for
safety you understand, but you've always been a quiet
and level headed chap so we're going to let you finish
out the day, if you could prep all your accounts to
hand over that would be great, and don't worry, we've
told security you're ok to stay past five if you need to.
Just remember, we *will* be writing your reference. I'm
afraid I've got to make a call now so I'll have to end
this meeting. Don't be a stranger, drop me a line when
you get set up somewhere else so we can touch base."

The door snicked shut behind Mike before he even
realise Daniels had stood up and escorted him out of
the room. He sank back against the door and found he
could make out Daniels call on the other side.
"Toby! Heard you had a bit of bad luck on the job
front, got caught with a bit of the old snorty snort.
Well good news, we have a position just opened up
here. Bit sad really, lovely fella and good at the work,
just didn't fit in, can you start tomorrow?"

Mike's foot touched base with the potted plant next
to the door frame and it smashed against the lift door
down the hall.

Mike was wandering aimlessly across the lobby
towards the exit muttering to himself, "Screw them,
reference or no reference I'm outta here." when Sharon
fielded him and shuffled him to the door where his
three o'clock appointment was waiting.

Mike opened the office door and his eyes fell across
a bull like gentlemen in a cheap black suit. He sat at
the desk holding a cup of tea and looked like he was
trying not to break the fragile china cup in his giant
paw of a hand. The open face below his bald head
broke into a beaming smile that crinkled his eyebrows
as he rose and offered his hand.

"Hello, my names Michael Simkind, how can I help
you Mr…?" Asked Mike taking the hand, which was

81

the firm bone crushing death grip he expected, and seating himself behind the desk as the customer sat back in his seat.

"Kev, good to meet you, and you can help me by lending me a hundred million quid Michael" replied the stranger as he leaned back, crossed his legs and folded his hands on his torso.

"I see, I assume you have done business with us before if you intend such a sizeable transaction?"

"Nope, first time here."

"Well I'm afraid we probably won't be able to help you, we could only make a business loan of that size to an existing customer or someone with an excellent track record or credentials, what's your business history?"

"Ah well, sorry to have wasted your time then, don't have much business history, just ten years as a self-employed entertainer. What would these excellent credentials be when they're at home?"

"That would be someone with, hang on, an entertainer, haven't I seen you somewhere?" Mike asked.

"You might have, you very well might have." Kev's grin got even wider.

"Yeah, yeah I'm sure I have. Didn't you used to eat tables on TV?"

"Yup, that was me, Kev the Post-Modernist Gastronome" Beamed Kev.

"Ok, I have to ask, what does a self-employed entertainer want with a hundred million pounds?"

"I've seen an investment opportunity. There's this old open cast pit out' back of ours that I reckon 'd make a good housing development, I need the money to buy it and turn it around."

"Hmm, that might actually be a sound investment, do you have experience in the development trade?"

"Nope"

Mike's brow furrowed "So how are you going to build houses on it?"

"I'm not" replied Kev happily "I'm gonna parcel it up and sell it to someone who will."

"Like the major building companies? Do you know any of them?" asked Mike leaning forward a little

"Nope."

"Ah, well, I do" Mike slumped back, deflated "and trust me, without having a contact there they won't talk to you, even if you do have the land."

"That's ok, I've got that covered" announced Kev with a grin "I'm just gonna hire someone who does"

"I see" said Mike "and the rules and regulations around this sort of business?"

"I'll just hire someone who knows all about that" said Kev. Mike was starting to wonder if there was something wrong with Kev, he didn't seem any the less optimistic despite the way the conversation was going.

"So, if other companies are going to be doing the building, and you're hiring people to do the bits you can't do yourself, which is all of it, what exactly do you bring to the table?"

"I bring the money" said Kev
"Well, yes, except you want to borrow that from us. Do you not see the flaw in this business plan? I assume you have a written business plan?"

"Not really seeing the flaw I'm afraid mate, can you point it out to me?"

"Well, your plan revolves around you being the capital for this business, only you don't have any capital." Replied Mike, trying not to sound like he was explaining something to a small child.

"Right, and your business revolves around lending capital to people who want to invest it but don't have their own doesn't it?"

"Err..." Mike felt like the conversation was starting to get away from him.

"If I'd inherited the money would you think this was a sound investment?"

"Well, yes, depending on the details."

"Or what if I'd done this kind of business with you before?"

"Ah well, you see" said Mike striking out for familiar territory "if that were the case you would have a strong track record and that would make it an investment rather than a gamble."

"Ok then, what if I knew one of the directors, played golf with him sort of thing, would that be the "excellent credentials" you mentioned earlier?" Asked Kev, still grinning.

"No, excellent credentials means, er," Mike's shoulders slumped and his voice became smaller "yeah, yeah that's exactly what it means, but I know that you don't otherwise you'd have gone straight to them instead of me."

"And if I'd gone to you and you turned me down you'd be fired, and if you accepted and it went bad then you'd be the scape goat and get fired anyway right?" Kev asked in a much more sombre tone than Mike had heard so far.

Mike just nodded.

"Doesn't sound like a fun job."

"Doesn't matter, just got canned anyway." Murmured Mike.

"Well then, you don't really have owt to lose by agreeing this loan do you?" asked Kev, brightening up.

"They could try to sue or prosecute me."

"How so? You just said that it would be a sound investment if I had the money or if I knew any of't big muckety-mucks so you're just doing your job by approving a sensible business loan right?"

"I said it would depend on the details though." Mike objected in flat, unenthusiastic tone.

"Well then, let me tell you all about the details!" replied Kev, rubbing his hands together with glee. The next three hours were a blur of numbers, documents, maps, facts and figures, all delivered with Kev's overpowering enthusiasm until Mike found himself signing the loan on behalf of the company almost without realising it. Kev had shaken Mike's hand and was just stepping out the door when he turned back and said:

"Say Mikey, you said you know some of them property developers, fancy a job?

Dinosaur
Sam Sharp

Dinosaurs died out because of stress. The crocodiles survived because they were calm. This is what they'd told Julia on the mindfulness course, therefore she was in bed. Being a calm crocodile. Aware that the day had begun around her but endeavouring to remain perfectly peaceful, perfectly content, perfectly - no. There was a dripping.

"Harry, the roof might be leaking again," Julia called. Drawn curtains prevented her from seeing if it actually had rained.

From the adjoining bathroom there came a reply of, "I thought we got some men in to fix that. It did get fixed, didn't it?"

"We certainly paid to have it fixed," replied Julia.

"Well, the garden looked dry when I let the dog out," said Harry.

"And did you have your glasses on?" Julia asked.

"Admittedly, no."

It would be a leak. Julia heard every drip as a taunt to their joint savings account. But money was not important, what mattered was to be tranquil, to be perfectly peaceful, perfectly content, perf-

RIBBIT RIBBIT RIBBIT!

Harry's phone erupted to the chorus of Amazonian tree frogs, making Julia jolt almost as high as a frog could hop.

"Change your damn ringtone!" She plunged her head beneath the bedsheets to see if a mindful state of existence was accessible with the outside world heavily muffled.

"It's my mum," said Harry.

Julia wished Harry's mother could be muffled, just a little.

"It'll be breakfast news again," he said. "There's always a story that upsets her or worries her or makes her panic buy milk. I shouldn't answer. It only encourages her. I'm not going to answer."

Harry's rambling lent Julia a break from attempting to be mindful, and she thought that if it had rained Amazonian tree frogs those drips from the roof might not be water but amphibians dropping in. Maybe that's what Harry's mum had seen on the news.

"Hi, Mum!"

"Fool," Julia cried, yet not muffled enough.

"No, Mum, she's just shouting at Twitter again. Twitter? You remember, the one with the hashtags? Oh, you don't." He sighed. "No, I'll explain." The bathroom door closed with a distinct kick, Harry's voice dull from the other side.

Beneath the sheets it began to get stuffy. Perhaps such warmth would help Julia relax, allow her to become perfectly peaceful and perfectly content while a cocker spaniel, swathed in mud, clambered up the foot of the bed and hid beneath the sheets with her.

"Laslow," said Julia, "this doesn't help find inner peace."

Laslow whimpered, which he wasn't prone to doing. Julia flung aside the sheets and saw him cowering.

"Why so spooked, dog?" She asked.

The bathroom door opened and out came Harry, dressing gown open and modesty unspared.

"If my mum ever asks again - which she probably will, - Twitter is the neighbours' pet parakeet and it eats hashtags. Why is there a very muddy Laslow in the bed?"

"He won't say. What did your mother want?"

"Apparently we've had localised flooding overnight and she was wondering if we're dry. I informed her we are."

"But that drip?" Julia pointed out.

"I told you, it looked dry when I let Laslow out. It's probably condensation."

"You didn't have your glasses on," said Julia. "And look at how muddy Laslow is - the garden must be flooded."

Harry began to fret. "The koi pond! Where are my glasses?" He hunted frantically.

Julia was surprised. "But we've never had any koi. It's just a pond."

"True," Harry replied, rifling through his sock draw, "but the filtration! A delicate balance of weeds, ruined! Now we'll never have koi. Where are my glasses?"

Outside, a bird began squawking. Julia reached under Harry's pillow and plucked out his glasses. "Here. And don't worry about the filtration, we'll buy new weeds," she reassured him.

Outside, another bird began squawking.

"These glasses are so smeared," said Harry. "And don't worry about the filtration?! Really, Julia."

Perfectly peaceful, Julia reminded herself. Harry could worry about pond weed but that wouldn't affect her, she wasn't going to be a distraught dinosaur. No, she was a calm crocodile.

Outside, many birds began squawking.

Harry marched for the window. "If those birds are eating my filtration weed, I-."

THUD, against the glass.

89

Laslow leapt from the bed and wriggled beneath it.

"A bird?" suggested Julia. Calm crocodile, she reminded herself.

Harry tentatively opened the curtains. A dazed bird stumbled about the window-ledge; upon seeing Harry it jumped off the edge and careened into a tree. Around that tree flew many birds, a flurry squawking in alarm.

"Bloody hell!" Said Harry. "There's a dinosaur in the garden. The garden's flooded and there's a dinosaur in it!"

Unbidden, Julia's eyebrow arched. "Clean your glasses," she said.

Harry removed his glasses, rubbed them with the belt of his dressing gown, then popped them back on. "Dinosaur," squeaked Harry. He then fastened together his dressing gown, modesty seemingly wanting to be spared when confronted with a dinosaur.

Julia rose to stand next to Harry. "Are you sure you're not-- Bloody hell," she said. "There is a dinosaur in the garden. And it's meditating."

Scratches
Ollie Francis

There is a roughness to the underside of your hands. Hard calluses and sandpaper skin mar the surface like stars in the sky. When you touch me, you leave marks — white lines of scratches across my arms and neck.

You speak of someone else — she shows an interest and you are flattered. You joke about it when you come home, half-heartedly, hoping that I won't care. Your eyes appeal to my compassion, my obsession, linger for a moment too long, looking for reassurance. Your head nods in false laughter at the absurdity of it — the ridiculous notion that another might stand a chance against me. As if, you giggle. As if.

These are all scratches of their own. The nick and scrape of guilt are the knives slipping across the heart of us. Every word of overactive confession comes with a score across the surface of our skin, threatening to burst our bubble. It is so much fear of losing me.

You have always been so beautiful. You never appreciated it. You only ever saw your rough hands and your weatherbeaten face. I only saw the hard work and the perseverance through pain. But when you look at me now, I see the tender flesh beneath, the desperation to be here with me now in the heart of intimacy.

You never understand that these are my scratches, my victory wounds. The pain you anticipate inflicting is the proof that I wait for. It is the moment of your return. It is evidence of your hand on me, me and only me.

The Baozi Inn
Helen Daniels

"Drugs."

"What?"

"I bet it's drugs," I stared at the metal table in front of me.

Ben caught the tennis ball he had been bouncing against the opposite wall. "I doubt it." He shrugged and went back to bouncing.

"Why?" I stared harder, trying to work out what that dark red cloth was covering.

"Well, drug dealers don't pay strangers to guard their stash, for one thing," Ben sighed. The ball bounced off the wall at an odd angle. He let it roll away and turned around. "And they don't tend to cruise Chinese restaurants either."

"How do you know?" I chewed my thumbnail to hide a smirk. "Do you do a lot of cruising?"

Ben raised an eyebrow at me. I looked away. "It was your turn fifteen minutes ago," I gestured to the Scrabble board in front of me.

Ben settled himself into the chair opposite, dark eyes narrowed to the board, fingers drumming on the table in thought. "Ah!" He added 'tison' to the 'jet' that I had laid down. "Jettison."

"Bastard."

He smiled smugly. "You're crap at this."

I grumbled and started rearranging my tiles in their holder.

"Connor," Ben said after awhile.

"Mmm?" I was still trying to make a decent word out of Q, R, T, I and P.

"Do you think it could be guns?"

I looked up at him. "Wrong shape," I said dismissively.

Ben snorted a little and shook his head.

"What? I was making an educated guess. Are you laughing at me?"

"No."

"Good. Don't." I frowned at the tiles, "I can't do anything with these sodding letters."

Ben leaned over the table. "Trip," he said after about ten seconds. "You really are awful at this game."

"Fine. I give up. I'm thick. Let's play something else."

"You don't need to get pissy about it," he grinned at me, "it's just a game."

I ignored him. "Where did the ball go?"

He glanced around the room. "Over there," he made a vague gesture towards some cabinets at the far side of the room. "How long have we got left?"

I checked my watch, "He said he'd be back in two hours and we've been here...forty five minutes, so, an hour and fifteen minutes."

Ben groaned and stretched his skinny arms over his head. "He'd best not leave us here any longer. I'm already bored out of my fucking skull and this place stinks of disinfectant or something."

"If you'd been nicer to me, we'd still be playing Scrabble."

"And if you'd been nicer to me, this whole evening would've turned out rather differently," he looked directly at me, "wouldn't it?"

"We can keep playing if you like," I said quickly.

Ben sighed heavily. "Fine."

I put my Q back and shook the bag around a bit. Ben seemed to be studying me, smiling with just one side of his mouth. "Can you please not do that?" I asked without looking at him. He shrugged and looked away. I let out a breath I didn't realise I'd been holding.

When the silence became oppressive, Ben said "I'm looking forward to my £200."

"You mean your £100," I picked some letters out of the bag, "we are splitting it 50/50, right?"

"If you say so."

"I do."

"Fair enough."

I sighed and put the bag of tiles back on the table. "Why shouldn't we split it 50/50?"

"I never said we shouldn't."

"You implied it."

"How?"

"Oh, piss off!"

He smirked. "You're in a bad mood to say you're about to earn £100 for doing absolutely nothing."

"Am I? Can't think why." I wasn't even trying to play Scrabble now. My head had started to throb and I clenched my jaw, making the pain arch and pulse across my temples.

Ben calmly leaned back in the old metal chair and stretched his legs up onto the table. There was a small hole in the sole of his expensive leather boot. He crossed his arms and stared right at me, his head on one side in mock concern. "What's wrong with you?"

"Nothing. I just don't feel good about this whole arrangement, alright? I wish you hadn't talked me into it, but hey, that's my fault, isn't it? I always let you force me into things. You're such a"

"I didn't force you," he said quietly. The chipped nail varnish on the fingernails of his left hand had suddenly become captivating.

"You didn't exactly give me a choice though, did you?" I affected a high and pathetic voice, "Yes sir, my friend and I will happily sit in a freezing cold kitchen for two hours. We'd love to help you cover up whatever the hell this is," my voice returned to normal "and yes, it does fucking stink in here."

"You could've buggered off and left me to it."

"Could I?"

"Yep."

"I should've, then."

"Yeah, you should."

"I'll leave now then, shall I?"

"Go ahead, but if you leave I'm not giving you your share."

I ground my teeth. My hands were shaking. I knew my stupid, freckly face had to have gone really red.

"You know what? I honestly don't care any more. Keep it. Keep your fucking money. I'm gone."

My chair screeched on the linoleum floor as I shoved it back and stomped over to the door. I knew I probably looked like a prat, which only made me feel worse. I grabbed the door handle hard and yanked. Nothing happened. I yanked again.

"It's locked."

"What?"

"It's locked. The fucking door's locked!"

"Ben swung his legs off the table and walked over to me. "Can't be."

"You try it then."

He pulled on the handle a few times. The door made metallic clinking sounds, but stayed shut. "Shit."

"He's locked us in here." I walked away from the door, rubbing my hair into messy ginger spikes, "we're trapped."

"Don't be a drama queen. The door's probably just a bit stiff, that's all," Ben shoved his shoulder against the door and pushed. Again, nothing happened. "Huh. I guess it is locked."

"You think?"

"Looks like you're stuck here 'till Sunglasses gets back after all," he shrugged, "Scrabble?"

"Are you not even a little bothered by this?" I widened my eyes at him, "I mean, a guy in a purple coat and sunglasses has locked us in a kitchen, for fuck's sake."

"Nah, he seemed OK."

I shook my head. "Mad. Completely mad." I walked away from the door muttering to myself.

Ben followed and wrapped his arms around me from behind. "You need to calm down," he told me, serious now. "You're scaring me."

I was still shaking my head slightly and staring at the floor. He hugged me tightly until I stopped fidgeting.

"There. Just relax. We'll be out of here soon, and then we'll never have to think about any of this again. We'll never go back to the Baozi Inn, I promise."

I took a deep, shaky breath. "We've only got an hour left," I said, trying to keep my voice steady.

"Exactly. Come on."

We sat back down again. I stared at the Scrabble board, feeling even less like playing now. What the hell was going on? Ben being so calm was actually making me feel more nervous, but I tried not to let it show. After awhile I noticed that his eyes kept flicking between me and the object on the table. I turned slightly so that I could look at it.

"I'm going to see what's under that cloth," Ben announced, standing up too quickly and making his chair tip over. It fell to the floor with a clang.

"Oh no, please don't," I whined, "we've only got fifty minutes left now."

"I want to prove to you that there's nothing worth looking at under there, then maybe you'll settle down." He sounded aggravated.

"Fine, go on then, but if he sees that you've moved it, he won't be impressed. He told us in the cafe not to touch it."

"He'll never know. I'm just gonna lift the cloth up a bit and have a peek."

"I don't think you should."

"Half an hour ago you wouldn't shut up about what could be under there and now you don't wanna know?"

"Yes. I don't want to know."

"You don't have to look with me."

I frowned.

"I won't tell you what I see."

"It's your decision."

He walked over to the table slowly. I didn't want to know. I didn't want to look. But as Ben's hand got closer to the cloth, I was transfixed. He took a deep breath to calm himself before peeling back the thick red material.

"Oh God," he dropped the cloth as if it had burned him and stumbled back from the table with his other hand across his mouth.

"What?" I asked, panicked, "What did you see?"

Ben coughed violently and shook his head.

"Ben?"

"No," he turned to face the kitchen sink and retched.

I wanted to help him, to offer some sort of comfort, but I felt pinned to my chair, too heavy to get up. Ben made his way back to me on shaking legs. He looked like hell; so pale he was almost translucent. His eyes looked entirely too dark for his face and his hair hung limply on his forehead, drenched with sweat.

"We need to leave," he said quietly.

"What's under there, Ben?" I made my voice sound firm.

Ben shook his head and moaned, running his hands through his hair.

"It's not drugs then? Or guns?"

He laughed without humour. "No, Connor. It's not drugs or guns."

"What is it?"

"I...Connor, I'm not saying, OK? If you wanna know so badly, fucking look for yourself."

I stood up. Did I really want to look now, given Ben's reaction? I walked over to the table with feigned confidence, hesitating only for a moment.

"Jesus."

There was a body on the table. Only, it wasn't a body in the traditional sense. This body was suspended in a tank of eerie green water. It's limbs weren't exactly attached to its torso either. Instead long red blood vessels and thin strings of muscle held them on a few inches away from where they were supposed to be, bobbing minutely. It was definitely a woman. Her eyes and mouth had been sewn shut with thick black cord. Slash marks and scars covered her entire form, and the skin in between was mottled grey, purple and green. I felt my stomach churn, but I couldn't look away from her. The tank seemed to have been specially made to fit. It followed the contours of her body with about three inches of space between her flesh and the clear plastic. The sickening smell of chemicals that filled the room had got worse. I felt my eyes water, a few tears sliding down my cheeks and dripping softly into the tank, creating tiny ripples.

"How the fuck can you look at it for that long?" Ben had got up from his chair. He sounded angry.

I turned to face him. "Her. She's a her, not an it. Show some respect."

"Respect? You're messed up, seriously."

"I'm messed up? She's the victim, you idiot. We shouldn't be afraid of her. We should be afraid of the people who put her here."

I picked up the cloth, planning to drape it over the tank again, but something stopped me. I just couldn't take my eyes off the body. I felt a drawn to her somehow.

Ben had acquired a fork from somewhere and was shoving it into the metal between the two heavy doors. They stayed locked.

"Shit!" Ben shouted, kicking the door. "What time is it, Connor? When the hell can we get out of here? And cover that fucking thing back up."

I glared at him. "We've got twenty minutes left." I made no move to cover the body again. Instead I walked over to the door, leant against it, and slowly sank down into a crouch. Ben gave up attacking the door with the fork and sat down next to me.

"He's not coming back. Sunglasses, I mean," his voice was very quiet.

"Why wouldn't he?"

"We're gonna end up like" he gestured to the tank.

I sighed through my nose. "Yeah, probably."

"£200 seems like fuck all now, in comparison."

"£100 each," I corrected.

Ben's eyes crumpled and he started laughing like a maniac. Tears streamed down his face and every other breath was a wheeze. "Christ," he choked as he got his breath back, "Jesus Christ this is weird."

I nodded sadly, "Just a bit."

"I wish we'd got a burger tonight instead of Chinese. I thought there was something weird about that damn cafe," Ben's eyes flicked quickly to the tank and then back to me. "You really shouldn't have been such a dick."

"Yeah. I know."

"Why are you so afraid all the time? All I wanted was"

104

"Stop."

"You didn't let me finish."

"Is there any point? Especially now?"

Ben squared his shoulders. "Nope. I guess not."

A few minutes later I uncurled myself and went back to the tank. I just had to be near it. I couldn't explain why. I heard Ben stand up, but he didn't follow me. I checked my watch. Five minutes. Reluctantly I pulled the cloth back over the tank and smoothed down the sides. Ben threw his fork in the sink. It made an angry noise.

I jumped, "Christ, you'll wake the dead with that racket."

"Don't say shit like that," he mumbled.

"Sorry," I smiled weakly, "poor choice of words."

"Hmm."

We sat in silence. Five minutes came and went. Then another five. Then another.

"Told you, he's not coming back.'

I head the grating, metallic sound of a key being turned in the lock. "You were saying?"

We both stood up and I started to pack away the Scrabble board

Sunglasses walked calmly into the room, purple trench coat swishing around his calves, an ugly smile splitting his face.

"Gentlemen, sorry for the delay. I was rather...encumbered."

I couldn't see his eyes beneath his sunglasses, but he turned his greasy head to each of us in turn.

"I trust everything went well?'

"Mmmhmm," Ben nodded and looked at the floor.

"Yep" I smiled weakly.

"Are you sure? You seem rather pale." He placed a hand on Ben's shoulder, long, painted nails digging into the material of Ben's jacket.

"What? Oh yeah. Yeah I'm fine. Had some bad chop suey earlier," Ben tried to laugh, but couldn't quite manage it. He just gulped instead. I dropped the bag of Scrabble tiles.

Sunglasses frowned, the oily skin between his eyebrows creasing into deep grooves. "You looked."

"What?" I couldn't quite keep the panic out of my voice.

Sunglasses glared at me. "You looked under the cloth."

"No, no. Honestly. Honestly we didn't," Ben was shaking his head repeatedly.

Sunglasses sighed again. "Why do they always look?" he said, mostly to himself. "Ah well."

He walked towards the door.

"Wait, you're not going to leave us here?!" Ben stumbled after him, but he was too slow. Sunglasses slammed the door in his face. The lock clicked and Sunglasses waved to us through the glass window, then he was gone.

Ben was pounding frantically on the door. "Hey! Hey you fucking shit! Let us out!"

I put a hand on his shoulder. He gave the door a final slam with both fists before falling into my arms.

The lights flickered and then went out.

A few moments later, I heard the heart sickening crash of falling water.

Baker's Meadow
Mark Delmonte

By the time Annabella had got back to the house the blood was already soaking through her dress. It was August, and the hot molten rays came dripping through the leaves of the sycamore trees that lined the street. Ginny had watched that tiny distant object thing turn into her daughter as it re-emerged over the top of the hill. She then dropped the tea towel she was using and ran to the door.

"He did it, he did it!" Bawled Annabella with livid indignation as she raised an accusing finger towards her elder brother Blake, who had wanted to reach Momma first but couldn't cos he was hobbling.

"Look what she did to me too!" He protested, pointing at a cut and swollen left knee.

Ginny took very little interest in who did what to whom and was much more concerned that the material around her daughter's mid-drift was dark crimson, and that she was beginning to appear faint.

"Blake, hush your mouth and run to the bathroom cabinet. I need a bandage quick."

It was as she said these words that Annabella lost consciousness.

Ginny was more than familiar with the route to the hospital. She knew where all the hazards were and what set of lights would be the most likely to delay her; normally the ones at the top of the hill by the brook where Sheriff Beolay would lie in wait for any drivers that came through over the speed limit. She hated to drive past that place where there was that shameful business of the sheep rustling and the all too contemptible attitude of Tommy Barrett firing up the neighbourhood about her Ritchie's drinking which drove her man to making these two half-orphans. But hey, old Tom sure got his come-uppance! And besides even if Ritchie did drink some he'd still come home...

But it was then that he would drive her out this way to the accident ward, drinking from the whiskey flask that he kept in the glove compartment and pleading her forgiveness – the numbness of her broken teeth and the blurring across her eyes would force her silence; a silence that Ritchie always took for compliance.

"Will they look at my knee too Mommy?"

Ginny didn't answer. She leant forward in her seat so that she could look both ways for traffic. She pressed hard on the gas as they approached the junction up past the brook. There was no sign of Sheriff Beolay.

At the front of the accident ward the shadows of the trees at the bottom of the valley had started to lengthen. The sun had grown ochre in its complexion and a tangerine moon hung new in the distance. The wailing of sirens and the rushing and rattling of passing hospital trolleys seemed only to deaden Ginny's nerves as she arrived at the reception desk carrying Annabella under her arm.

"Please remain calm Miss Hillyard and we'll do our very best to get your daughter looked at as soon as possible. I can't do anything to help you whilst you're shouting at me. I need to find a consultant who is free. Now take a seat and someone will be available shortly."

The familiar smell of polished floors and alcohol-based liniment accompanied the gathering of the wounded and unwell that slouched before her. She continued to press her hand onto Annabella's wound which by now had stopped bleeding. Blake sat cross-legged in front of her tracing a finger along the pattern of the tiles.

"Could Miss Hillyard please come through."

Doctor Reynolds was a tall inelegant man who wore thick glasses upon a pockmarked face dominated by a bulbous nose and hairy nostrils. "Nice to see you again Miss Hillyard, What in the hell happened here?"

"She fell on some wet grass out in the backyard whilst carrying some logs." She said as she ran her fingers through Blake's hair and kissed him on the forehead.

"What's a child her age doing carrying logs?" He alternated his gaze between the top of his rims and the lenses that made his eyes appear huge.

"Can't stop'em from doing anything they wanna do Doc. She sees her Momma carrying logs and she gets right up and tries to do the same. Sometimes there just ain't nothing I can do about it."

"Well it looks like a couple of stitches should do it. I suggest that in future you try to exert some more control over your children Miss Hillyard."

Outside the treatment cubicle, the corridor of the accident ward had become ghostly quiet. Back at the parking lot Annabella fell asleep in her mother's arms. Up ahead there was a flashing light and the vague glimmer of a Police badge. It was Sheriff Beolay.

"Howdy Miss Hillyard, how you doin?"

"Why I'm pretty good as always sheriff. How you doin?"

"Pretty good too ma'am. I'm sorry but I need to converse with you about an earlier incident involving two young children."

Blake hid behind his Mother to escape the Sheriff's leaden stare.

"And what incident might this be Sheriff Beolay?"

"Well perhaps if you'all could just step into my car then I can ask a few questions."

With a nod from his mother Blake reluctantly poked his head into the back of the car, and dragged his body along behind it into the far corner. Ginny, still carrying a very sleepy Annabella, followed him.

"Sir, I have a rather sickly child with me so if you'd be so kind as to…"

"Ma'am, I rather hoped that with the recent tragedy of a Mr Richard Brookes that your domestic problems would now be over, but it appears that a little bit of what these new psychologists call 'learnt behaviour' is creeping into your household. I have it on good authority that a knife was used on your daughter in order to try and placate her during some horseplay over by the stream. Were you aware that your son carries a knife?"

"You followed me all the way up here to the General hospital to tell me that Sheriff Beolay? Why what boy doesn't carry a penknife these days?"

Blake started to cry.

"Why I'm afraid that this is no ordinary penknife Miss Hillyard. There was a reliable witness to this afternoon's unseemly episode. Tommy Barrett, driving past in his tractor called on me to recover the blade which he saw young Blake here drop as he gave chase to Annabella. The serrated edge matches exactly that which was used to cut the throats of a couple of his sheep up over at Baker's Meadow last week. Appears that she started shouting stuff about it and was threatening to tell you when Blake pinned her down and threatened to cut her from head to toe. According to Barrett she had to smash a rock across his leg to escape."

Blake gazed silently at two Jackdaws that were pecking at each other on the metal gate-post by the entrance to the parking-lot.

"Now I'm afraid that I'm now going to have to lock you all in the car and drive back to the station for further questioning. It might be as well to prepare young Blake here for a lengthy stay."

Islands Far From Home
Gareth Madgwick

She comes to see me now, "*Avó!*" she cries as she
runs into my room, scattering the ornaments, little
figures of Christ and sheet music. They were piled onto
the sterile, white surfaces of my room and float up,
swept by Antonia's entry, slowing to the apex of their
flight and drifting back down as fading, crumbling
leaves of an old existence. She has known only this
gravity all of her life. I remember the feel of Earth, the
crunch of sand, of dirt and of leaves underfoot.

I drop my guitar to the floor, letting it fall softly
and hold Antonia as she jumps up to me, her arms
around my neck. She's a teenager now, like the rest of
her generation. They and their mothers and fathers
grew up in these steel tubes with the blackness of space
outside. There is no sunlight out here, there hasn't been
for decades. It faded with my youth as we journeyed
out of the solar system. We should tell these children
what life was like where we came from and how the
world really worked.

"How are you? What have you been doing?" I ask
as she throws herself down to the floor, onto the

striped yellow and red rug that I brought with me from home.

"Studying," she says, sullen now, "It's so dull,"
She never used to look like this. Children seem to loose their sense of excitement and wide eyed gaze as they grow. I suppose they need to in order to become adults.

"But we all need to study don't we? So that we can work at what we want to when we arrive. You'll have you whole life ahead of you when we get there, and so much to do," I think back to the thrill that I had when we set off. The possibilities that expanded ahead of us. The families to raise and nurture. The new society to forge.

"The men say I have to match with Patrick when we arrive"
Match? Is that what they're calling it now?
"When did you find this out?"
"Father told me when he got back from the meeting last night,"
Father. I remember when Antonia's father was a little boy himself, running through the corridors of the *Vasco da Gama* in his unique low gravity gait, avoiding chores and his parents and wanting only to play with the rest of the children. Back then the ship was filled with laughter and play. Now he is prostituting his own daughter.

"And what do you think? What do you want to do?" I ask Antonia
She shrugs and looked away, as if it didn't really matter.

How did we get here?
Pedro and I went deep into the jungle in Amazonas once, searching for new species. We found some, photographed, videoed and recorded them for posterity. We took some dead insects and some blood from the larger animals, like the lizards. That night, we toasted our success with wine from a plastic bottle in plastic glasses, the guides around us cursing their

warm beer. We thought then that we had found something incredible, something that no one else had ever seen. That bug had bitten us strongly and would hold us for the rest of our lives.

We couldn't let go then, we stared at the canopy, lit green even at night by our own generators, but beyond it, the stars, they looked so far away then, as the insects darted around and across the moon.

"They'll be gone soon," said Pedro on another expedition years later. The wine working its way into an already morose heart. "As fast as we find these specimens they are being wiped out,"

I had nodded, knowing that he was right. The world we had devoted ourselves to was being destroyed around us. That first patch of rainforest we had started out in so many years earlier was already a logging plantation. The species we had found were long gone.

Our university was looking for volunteers to join the *Vasco* that year. I remember making the application when we got back home, telling Pedro that *we* were going, or at least that *I* was going and I'd find someone to play his role. I said that if he didn't want to go, I'd bury him in the back yard and take a look-a-like. I was half joking.

I leapt for joy when we were accepted, hugging Pedro and letting our tears mingle. To know that we were going out there, to a world circling another star, where we had gazed all those years before was the essence of joy, a feeling that I could only express with whoops and hollering, a primal thrill.

I remember meeting the other couples that had joined the voyage, the Russians, the Americans, the Indians and the Chinese. Politics, governments and corporations had picked us all. All the contributing parties wanting to send their best to make sure that if the whole crazy venture was a success then it would be a success because of them. The excitement of the group was real though. Our hands were shaking as we grasped each other's tentatively then developing into huge group hugs. We were truly stepping into the unknown.

That was then.

"What do you want to do, when we get there?" I ask, searching for a glimmer, a glint, panning for gold in muddy waters.

"I'll do the farming I suppose,"

"But what do you *want* to do?"

She looks at me as if she doesn't understand the question. Her face wrinkles confused.

"I have to go now *Avó*, I have to go to the gym," She stands up, one last glance over her shoulder, and then walks off down the corridor, her long, lolloping strides causing her shoulders to rise and fall slowly as she does so.

I lean down and pick at my guitar again, letting the chords come slowly, not really paying a lot of attention to what I play, my fingers picking their way through the notes.

I had brought it with me, we were all allowed to bring a few small items, favourite clothes, keepsakes. Everything else was provided for us. As we watched our tiny green and blue marble getting smaller and smaller, I hugged it to me.

"Play," Pedro had said, I did and I sang.
The old explorers, they had a type of music for times like this, when they were far from home and may never see it again. *Fado.* We knew that we would never see home again. To us, home was being destroyed, piece by valuable piece, to keep the billions and billions of people alive.

Those old explorers used to sing of their explorations, their visits to lands and islands and their hopes to return, their sadness at being far from their loved ones. We took our loved ones with us, knowing we would never see home. Our islands are each our own. We have come to them and each inhabit that place to our selves. Love has no place now.

I sang a song back then, of loss and home. But there was hope tinged in it, hope that we would find something greater, that we would arrive on a world that we could call our own, and begin again, over fifty years later.

There were so few of us then in the enormous ship, sailing on our way, with so many empty rooms to explore. We shrieked like small children as we scampered around it. Hugging each other, throwing our arms around people that, before the launch, were complete strangers. We knew, by the end of our voyage, the *Vasco Da Gama* would be full of our families, all growing up together in hope and happiness.

How did we forget?

I lay the guitar to one side, and stretch out on my bed, empty now, but for my own, failing body. I remember climbing trees, almost like yesterday. Our time on the *Vasco* seems like a dream, as if, one day, we will wake up, and then everything will be as it was before.

I hate Pedro now for what he did. For what they all did. For what they all still do. He hadn't even told me at first. He treated me like he treated the children, the poor girls of that second generation that they controlled, owned and ruined. He and the rest of the men, kept themselves in their own little committees and their own little meetings. We had started out as one little community, but the men were meeting by themselves, "Just to talk like men," That's when they must have started this.

I felt isolated. Pedro was my greatest friend back home. Compared with him I had little in common with the other women on the Vasco. I was attracted to biology by the sense of wonder it brought to me. They seemed attracted by the need to categorise and control it all. Their approach left me cold and I retreated to my own lab and my own bedroom, working along on the periodicals and studies that drifted down the radio waves towards us.

He took Christina one day, our own daughter.

"Where are you too going?"

"Anton's," A glare shot in my direction. He had long stopped giving me full answers to my questions. Anton had no children. He was a minor scientist from the Russian contingent.

"Why?" I asked stepping towards him, I was tired of his secrecy but left him to it, thinking that whatever he was doing, it no longer bothered me if it made no difference to my own life. He turned away.

"Pedro!"

"Wait outside," he said to Christina, ushering her out of the door. He turned to me then.

"The men need to start her off, that's where she's going," I darted towards him and he put his hands up as I did so, pushed me backwards, "She's one of the last girls. All the others have done it. Don't worry, they're not rough,"

I launched myself through the air, my hand drawing to slap him backhanded. The satisfaction I felt from catching him full in the face was short lived.

"Bring her back in,"

He shook his head.

"Please, don't make a fuss. This is what we are doing now. You'd know from the others if you bothered to speak to them,"

"They can't accept this. This can't be what you all want,"

He looked at me then, and just for a second, I saw the old Pedro that I had fallen for. He looked afraid, as if someone was watching over his shoulder. Then his face cleared. It was the last time that I ever felt anything but hatred for him.

"This is the way it needs to be. We need to make sure that this all comes easily and naturally to them. Otherwise, our community will whither and die. The governments didn't put enough thought into this. They just hoped it would all work out, but we've been doing the sums. We need as much reproductive activity as possible,"

"Your daughter," I screamed. My eyes were filling with tears, I pushed against him, trying to get past, trying to get to her.

"We've studied animals all of our lives," he said, "This is how animal communities bind themselves. Look at bonobos,"

Look at Hyenas I thought, with their matriarchal hierarchy. Don't use my own speciality against me "We are not," I screamed at him, "chimpanzees. We are humans, we are *better*,"

One final push against me, and he was outside the door. I heard the lock click. I punched the code. Red light. I punched it again. The same. He had changed the codes. I could no longer leave my own rooms.

Now, I'm not sure that we are any better than animals

Did we fight them? Of course. There was no way that I would leave this to happen to my daughter again, or to my granddaughters. I was full of righteous fire and I knew that I was right. I got out of that damn room eventually and got together with Mei, Parvinder, Jess and the others. Jess lead us to the men's meeting and we stormed in. She said "Enough". Grabbed their secret plans laid out on the tables and hurled them into the garbage disposal.

For that, they spaced her. Put her in the airlock and opened it, letting her float away. She's still out there now, another piece of space junk from this terrible mission. Maybe if we'd tried again. Maybe if we'd done more. They couldn't have spaced all of us. We should have had the courage to try again and again to stop them. Instead, we hid ourselves away, those of us that still cared. We hid ourselves in our dreams in this long sleep between two worlds and simply hoped that the nightmare would end.

121

We are so far out now, our communications take decades to get home and back. What happens now is our concern, no one else's. It is the concern of just the men, women and children on the *Vasco*. We do nothing. I do nothing. I did nothing at the start, and it got worse, and worse, and now my Antonia, my granddaughter...

Have they got to her yet? How did we let this happen?

The worst of it is, the very worst, they have no idea, they just accept it. For her, all of this is normal. Floating around the air like a leaf, watching nothing but fifty year old web series, reading nothing except on a screen. No leatherbound, hardback, beautiful books, with pages that you run your hand down and sniff like the ones I remember. All of that sterility is normal. In the same way, they just accept how they are treated by the older men who pair them off when they have had their fill. They accept it like all the other weirdness that goes with being out here. We thought we had left the worst of the world behind us, instead, we have left the best.

Antonia comes again the next night.

"Why did you ask what I want to do," she says, hugging her knees to her chest, staring at me with her big, brown eyes. They remind me of her father, and her grandfather.

"Because that's what we did back home, we did what we wanted to,"

"Is that how you destroyed Earth?"

I look away, scared that she is right. "Some of us didn't want that, but not enough, not nearly enough," We sit in silence.

"*Avó*,"

"Yes?"

"Why do you never play your guitar for me?"

"Because, I play my guitar for me,"

"Play me something, please?"

So I do, I pick at the strings, cautiously at first, then with more confidence. I start, falteringly, to sing. I sing for her, not for me, but for her. I sing of where we came from, of the hopes we had, of the pain I feel when I see what happened to those hopes, to the dream of humanity become the misery of our life. Yet, I sing of the hope that remains, because, if she wants to hear me sing then maybe, one day, she will sing herself.

Thank you for reading.

- Bank Street Writers